Chaise

Printed in the United States of America.

Published by Offense Mechanisms.
www.offensemechanisms.com

ISBN-10: 0-9774110-6-0
ISBN-13: 978-0-9774110-6-1

Cover design by Paul Hughes.

Chaise

by Becci Noblit Goodall

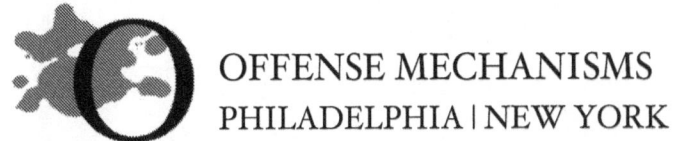

OFFENSE MECHANISMS
PHILADELPHIA | NEW YORK

Chaise is dedicated to my mentor and advisor at Juniata College, Judy Katz. She epitomizes the strength and power one person can extend to another. She was the first person to believe in my talent. A dedication on a page seems paltry compared to the ways in which she has changed my life.

I enjoy writing that merges fiction with reality. My experiences color this story, but *Chaise* isn't autobiographical (although I am lazy enough to sit on my couch for years). Most of the stories in this work begin at a starting point of something that happened to me, then they take off into something wildly fictional.

Advertisements have been culled from various celebrity and fashion magazines as well as the web and television. A nod goes out to Adbusters Magazine for showing me how to warp an ad for my own purposes.

Quotes from the 1960s hippie revolution were found in the coffee table book *Hippie* by Barry Miles.

Thanks to editor Paul Hughes. His genius and ability to find my innumerable inconsistencies made this book a readable work.

—Becci Noblit Goodall

TAPE 1
SIDE A

I live on my couch because I want to believe in magic. Pan roasted turkeys. Marriages that stick. Cookies that don't. Dads who disappear in one episode but return in the next. It's sort of like a Christmas Eve special when the fake Santa is drunk and you don't have faith, but you wait up anyway because you want to believe in something other than folded Gap turtlenecks and shrink wrapped Baby Phat.

"I believe I'll wait," you say.

You do a shot every time Cindy Lou Who says "who." You feel sorry for the Grinch because he doesn't have presents and his heart is small. And so it goes. Then one day you see that unused gifts are all there ever was, but you keep working to fill the space. And your heart constricts. Attacks. So there you are, hanging upside down on the monkey bars. The sky is blue. Your Hubba Bubba mouth chews out words like Tonka Truck, Schwinn Bike, Cabbage Patch Dolls. Knees slide from the rung. You fall chest-first to the ground. The air gets knocked out. You suck and suck but there is nothing. The bell rings. Recess is over. You come to on a gurney or in a padded room and you think to yourself *I was closer to the clouds upside down.*

The whistle blows.
You blot a bubble test.
The whistle blows.
You take the SAT.
The whistle blows.
You index reports.
Your files collapse.
The whistle blows.
You spill onto the tarmac.

Things go upside down.

Your skin turns blue.

And it is OK. good. At least the clouds are visible and you can put down the razorblade.

So begins the day of all days.

And this is how it started. It. This day that melds into the lexicon gibberish of the next. And you're not sure what chunk of minute turns that corner of Monday into Tuesday. One day. It's all one big long fucking day.

My Moleskine says it's been 156 weeks since I lay down on these velvet cushions. 26,280 hours since I pasted on this dead Elvis smile. 9,608,000 seconds of tapping away at this couch lair. I am a leather-tailed beaver gnawing my own fibula into branch tunnels.

The hole in the wall is clouded with moss and beaded teeth. I put pieces of me under pillows for fairies and lovers.

Every day I think about all the nailing and sitting. I think about Dr. Bob Jones, who can't help me. I think about my mother, who tells my aunts that I'm actually a missionary in India working to convert Hindus. I think about Jerry and Dan from Kelley's Pub, drinking Jaeger. I think about Heather and Rosalie from Juniata, questing to sell pheromones and change the world.

My friends used to call every day but right around the second year, they dropped down to only ringing on holidays. Their messages warbled into my background like cracked 8-tracks and Chaplin movies. They weren't real. Nothing was real but the additions to my couch. The fluffing of cushions and the newfound ability to stick to a solitary goal of never getting off.

I hammer shelves along the back chintz section and I think.

I think about the way I don't miss getting flipped off on I-95 or skipped in line at Whole Foods.

I think about the unfortunate lives of my kids. I imagine they say, "Poor mom, crazy mom, poor her." Then they turn to eat white pizza with Rolling Rock. Do they pretend I exist outside? Maybe they explain me to new lovers who will not understand a mother who has been sitting on a couch for three years. Maybe four.

She's a voluntary psycho. A 302 commitment. I bet that's what they say.

This is what I mull at 5 a.m., in the ass-crack of my life. The holding pattern I have chosen spins circles and laps up layers of ventricle and knuckle. I see shark fin implosions. I flip on the movie *Jaws* just to see the way girls and boys get chewed and stuck between huge plastic Spielberg teeth. I see that. What it feels like to be flossed out for the next scene.

If only I could stop thinking so much. I mash every little thing into rice dust.

How is a cereal box big enough to hold the Cap'n Crunch maze?

I can't stop.

I have mental Tourette's. But worse. Like that. Screams mean nothing beyond the sound bounce, which is why I think myself into corners. And I can't see a way clear of this un-blued place. This triangle will require body surfing if I decide to step out.

Fake fat, botulism lips, and boob jobs. Henry Kissinger, Descartes, and Pac-Man.

I want to create a Camel philosophy. I will sit here until I'm the new think tank IT KID. I wonder if they smoked some kind of camel butt shit in the desert to keep warm. Is that where the idea of Camel cigarettes originates? I mean, who the fuck sat there in some ad agency or smoke factory and said, "Camels—let's do camels"?

A frustrated salesman? I suppose.

I get the Marlboro cowboy thing. The slinky-sex Virginia Slims thing. Yes. But Camels? I don't get the connection.

Camels hump what they've hoarded. They plod on forked hooves. Survive sandstorms. Where is the smoke link? The hazy thing I'm missing? I think this as I curse my Harley lighter, which I'm always losing. I scrounge with my pinkie toe.

Yeah, a camel in a tuxedo with hooves crossed like arms. Call up *Vogue*, *Cosmo*, *Playboy*. Full-page ads.

I'm sold.

I imagine being humped under Joe Camel's fur like a ball of rubber cement—each layer stickier and dirtier than the last. My legs and eyelashes fade in the slow whiskered pucker. He sucks. There is no water. Next rest area: seven hundred ninety-nine miles.

No tents.

No oasis.

He drinks me from a striped accordion straw that winds from his mouth to my bellybutton. A reverse umbilical cord. Body parts clump the folded straw and it grows fat in the center like Bavarian donuts full of lard and sugar. He pulls and gnaws at me like Laffy Taffy. Purple nipples give way as all my good parts slide past his Adam's apple. What's left in the IV pouch is chunky like tin can chicken, which tastes somewhere in the middle of tuna and salmon.

Bargain food.

Buy one, get one free.

A chocolaty piss leaks from my face into the armrest. I drip onto the tongue and groove floor like evaporated milk, sticky with pumpkin pies and cheesecake.

Cellulite juice.

The phone rings.

Beeps.

Takes a message.

It's Mom again.

She raps the door in the hall. Knowing I won't let her in. This armrest is at least four feet from the door. She's crazy to think I'm getting up to let her in.

She calls up from the lobby.

"Beep me in. I've got beef stew."

I've never liked beef stew.

I buzz her up and scribble on a fuchsia Post-it note: 1. camels. 2. google.com. 3. lung cancer.

I realize my obsessions are weird.

I can't focus on Mom-gobble, so I don't. She sets the TV table up in front of me with the food. I blow her a kiss. She leaves.

The TV is stuck on seven. The god channel. Somewhere in behind the sound stage, men are practicing their Jesus speeches. I like the matinee performance.

I get up and skulk along the wall in the shadow of my couch. I have to pee. The need drives me to cushions I've lined along the wall. As long as my feet don't touch down, I'll be OK. I skulk to the bathroom. Never touching the floor.

Skulk. Skulk. Skulk. I love that word. It's in *Four Weddings and a Funeral*. So realistic. Love in four episodes. Death in between. And laughter.

My shoes screech and creak. I sort of hate crawling to the bathroom in these leather metal boots. The floor sweats beneath the pillows. It's clammy with fever. I paid $6000 for this tongue and groove in '92 when everyone was doing the hardwood-natural thing. We all joined Greenpeace and then put in pine floors so we could meditate on saving nature.

It's such a pain in the ass. Crawling. Staying as far off the ground as possible. Clinging to my loveseat back.

TAPE 2
SIDE B

Fashion is wondrous Fun in Mary Jane's Let's Play collection! Colorful happy cottons with embroidered play motifs; designed by Betty Barker, America's foremost designer of little girl fashions! Sizes 3 to 6x. About $5.

—Mary Jane Dresses
1350 Broadway, New York, NY
1948

As soon as I build a bigger couch, this will be unnecessary, but for now, I wobble across the couch cushion bridge in six-inch platform boots, which I got for $250 at Bobbi Jo's Leather and Lace Boutique on Fritkin Street. The saleslady said they were worn at a Jersey concert by the originally-original hair band KISS. Clown face and testosterone. Yeah, baby, yeah.

Normally I don't wear shoes but yesterday I felt myself drifting, as if my skin could no longer hold me in, so I built a wall with all the shoes I've ever owned. I lined them around my couch in a heel-to-heel circular stack. When they got over four pairs high, there was a fear of tumbling, so I strung phone cable in and out of the arches and toe holes. Huge knots anchor my fortress of soles.

It's a weird stability, having my life strung together by shoes. It reminds me of a Druid fortress. Something you'd wander through in bluish moonlight. Maybe slit your wrist for pink lemonade and climb out refreshed. And you would feel on top of the world until you saw the cops there outside the barrier. Stonehenge belongs to the public. Do not touch. Pay five quid to see. And you scream and scream, "But these are my rocks! I was born here... This is my home." So you run. Leap into a parking lot full of cars and realize that the mystery of life is just a tourist trap.

I got these heavy metal boots from the south end of the wall, third down to the left by the sandals and clogs. I found them among the seventies and eighties shoes, which I have tissue-wrapped into filing boxes. *These Are the Days of Our Lives*.

You could say it was a fetish or you could say it was the thing that kept me alive. The way I bought sandals instead of toilet paper. Pointy buckled boots before vegetables. There was no rhyme. No reason to the charging of soles. I had six closets jammed with pairs and pairs.

Now I label everything because I'm going through a neat phase. It won't last. And I don't recognize myself this way. It's not natural.

Going... Going.

Gone. F is for the clear plastic spikes that have fish painted onto the soles. P is for the cowboy boots with the round silver and turquoise buckles. The toes are squared off for kicking. I puked up Jack Daniels many times during that urban cowboy phase of riding mechanical bulls. My hips were full of volt and electric. Plug me in for Juicy-Juicy Couture.

Thank goodness for the clogs. Each one is my story. Without them, I might forget that hazy time of 1979.

I even have the yellow rubber galoshes from kindergarten, when I fell in love with Mrs. Cooper. She wore red velvet platforms. I wanted to be her so badly. Goddamn. I never got them, but I did get some red rubbers to protect my saddle shoes. You could jump in the mud and never get your church shoes dirty, which was crucial.

The patent leather Mary Janes are on the windowsill. I've planted cannabis and aloe between the buckles. Every few days I scrabble across a plank that balances from the couch back to the window seat so I can water living things.

I also have special silk red platforms like the ones Mrs. Cooper used to wear on Wednesdays, which she said was her night out with her husband. She was four-foot eleven and those sandals took her all the way up to five-foot four-something. I don't remember what I learned in that class.

Finger-painting? Long and short vowels? Who knows? I was thinking that if I could just wear those shoes, I'd grow up. If only, then, I'd understood why her scent made me squirm. It wasn't roses. It was more like earth dirt and stone. No. Or honeysuckle. Hot in the sun. I'd smell her and get goose-bumps to the ends of my pigtails and in my knee bends.

Tulips and chalkboards.

One day Mrs. Cooper said she liked my striped denim jumper, so I wore it every Wednesday.

What ever happens to kindergarten teachers?

I wonder. This is how I spend my days. I wonder and I draft plans for the couch extensions. Living room forecast. 70 degrees. All stations go. No immediate plans for travel.

Mom says that if I'm going to sit here and rot that I should at least sell off some of my shoes. She says I could feed the poor with the profits or donate to one of the poor stores. Now what in hell would Goodwill do with my sweet shoes? And how would my girls breathe?

She doesn't know me. She never knew me. That would be like giving away my heart to the witch in the candy cane house. I can't have a stranger editing my fairy tale.

I've tried to explain feng shui a million times.

Never wear lived-in things.

This goes here.

That goes there.

Marching in a high school band. Stepping in time. Beat. Beat. Crash. Run. Touchdown.

Push-'em-back-shove-'em-back-away-back. A cheer.

I put on my shoes when I need to feel alive.

St. Michael's. Lou's Cappuccino. Peggy's Place. Motel 6. Greece. The Miami Nutcracker Ballet. I-95. Step aerobics at Bali's. Abortions at the Front Street Clinic. Women's Lit. 302. A Streetcar Named Desire. Brunch at Martha's. Finger-fucking under the Halifax bleachers. Jaws II. Entry Level positions. The Dania head shop. Dylan at the Jazz Fest.

I don't know how to put this to understanding. To diagram what no one gets about this sit in. All I can say is that I walked before crawling. It feels like I've skipped crucial moments of absorption. My lips can't open wide enough to gulp the swirl back inside. It's all here. In my cowboy boots. Each loopy swirl winds into the next. And I have to know where it ends and until that happens I'm not getting up. Doing so would be disastrous.

So I don't go out anymore. The last time was a disaster. There was a buzz so furious in my thick head that I missed a client and a lover. I remember it best in the black Prada pumps. The salesman and the drummer.

The one with Dow Jones connections, the other with a Cadillac penis.

The one, the one, the one.

Agent Smith and Neo.

TAPE 3
SIDE A

A leader is one who can do things better, easier, and faster than others can do them. He knows a great deal and understands a great deal; and with his knowing and doing, he has the power to make people like him. A leader is selected by his followers.
—Children's Activities for Home and School
copyright 1948 by Child Training Association, Inc.
Chicago, Illinois

So here I am—here on my couch, which I have circled around everything I own. I guess maybe it's hard to picture the boredom of living life on a couch. But really, it's an adventure. Think of a sailing around the world in a cramped sailboat or sliding down the Nile in a houseboat. It's all there. It's all here. In my head.

What started out as just an ordinary couch has turned into a misshapen Peter Pan lookin' thing. I just kept adding things on. First, I had Derek help me rope the fridge, computer desk, and stove together so that they were connected to the La-Z-Boy armrest. This was necessary because I had to eat and pee. I'm not an invalid. I just want to stick to something for once in my life until it's done.

I tried to fashion my coach boat without touching the floor. At first, it was difficult and I have to admit to falling on the hot lava floor a couple of times. But for the most part, it never happens anymore. This obsession is so much simpler than the others. *Only date blond men. Only drink soy lattes. Only write on linen with pencil.* **Don't get on the floor.**

At first it was a goal. Now it's become survival. I can't be down there. I have this feeling that the floor will snag me. People are always talking about falling through cracks as if there is some black hole. *Poor John, the school just let him fall through the cracks...* Disappearing isn't the problem. Sticking between the fitted boards is the problem; getting your legs amputated in half-inch spaces, now that's an issue.

Some days I lie and lie here. Today, for example, I won't lift my head from these pillows because that means I will have to flip through infomercials about facials and back massagers that are mysteriously penis-shaped and pink. Three-bean casseroles and everlasting vibrators. The meaning of life.

So for now I inhale the non-filtered fuzz of their god. It's a round-the-clock saving of souls and budgets. The occasional missionary with fluffed-out mullet hair and blue eyelid wife tells about saving natives and starving potbellied children, none of whom ever seems to eat.

I stay here because there is a man I hate on the five o'clock broadcast. I love to hate him; it brings meaning to my day. He is this preacher salesman guy with fluffy coiffed hair kinda like a wedding cake doll. Sculpted. His biceps are a spectacular sales tool as he hawks Jeremy Ron's *How Would Jesus Cook?* cookbook.

Fat-free recipes and, best of all, the missionary section, which shows you how to change spicy native foods into American milk-and-macaroni cheese dishes. He talks a lot about virgin olive oil and the lubrication of things. Apparently, the path to eternal health can be found by braising with this Middle Eastern oil kit. He will explain these mysterious properties of life in the book. He takes MasterCard, Visa, debit, Discover, and cash money. Just one payment of $76.95 or four of $25.95.

There are no free knife sets or lettuce spinners. Just the book and the virgin oil. The extra money is used for pamphlets, Bibles, and the English clinic for teaching English in Bangladesh (Who can understand what they want if they can't speak our language?). It's logical, really, if you think it through.

Jeremy smoothes his thousand-dollar jacket and rubs his silk tie over taut abs. He is the smart guy preacher in a weird good cop/bad cop sell job. The other preacher acts dumb and flabby so that Jeremy can patiently explain the potluck good this oil project will generate. I wonder if they have air-conditioned poodle doghouses like Jim Bakker from the '80s.

Both have the Alabama/Texas accents because it is easier to drawl out heeehlllll and heaaaven slow-like. I grew up on this stuff. Personally, if I were the producer, I'd throw in some Jersey preachers or maybe a Boston accent. Heah is the way to gawd.

The script calls for a nod. Pastor John waggles his head and tears up. Clears throat.

Dormant lymphoma tweaks at my neck. I feel a snaky growing. A returning of chemo and radiation.

I throw a blob of hummus at the TV and the grainy spot makes a weird pirate eye-patch for the brother. I want to wipe the smear, but it is too far to stretch, to move, to clean. Madeline will have to remove it tomorrow after she cooks the Tuesday meal of whole-wheat spaghetti. Twenty-four noodles and a pot of calamari. Melted butter. Angel hair pasta.

Exactly two weeks ago, the brothers introduced this new youth pastor named Chandelier. No last name, just the first like a Madonna or a Cher. As if he were born a rock star.

Definition: chandelier: light, a light, a swinging crystal. Hangs from the ceiling.

He was clean-cut with a ribbed T-shirt and baggy cargo pants. Kind of a combination scientist/skater. It was a manu-factured cool-cool. Like boybands, but for church. A Chris-tian punk rock cool.

He was sitting in a shadowy room. The camera zoomed on his face in a zip shot. I got the sensation of vertigo, like I had to grab the edge of the couch to avoid pitching onto the carpet. To keep steady, I watched nothing but his lips and thought *This isn't real... This isn't real... Can this be real?*

Usually I don't take the God Channel seriously; it's more like a variety show or a comedy hour. Something equally sin-ister and funny at the same time. Maybe like watching a cannibal munching on baby bones and then getting a laugh when he trips and the elbow joint sticks up his nose. Something like that.

This day was different. I was mesmerized by Chandy (that's what he said to call him for short, so I do) as he took his electronic audience for a virtual tour of his newly refurbished haunted hell house in Bacon, Georgia. I remember thinking it was only July. Seemed a bit early for Halloween, which made me think of candy.

So I called Derek for some butterscotch Dum Dums. The little ones they gave at drive-through bank windows until hard candy became a liability.

I hung up the phone when I heard this retching and yelping coming from the screen. I sat up and there was this amateur lying on a hospital bed, puking up what looked like cottage cheese and ketchup or lumpy orange Russian dressing porridge. All mixing with a snotty nose flow. Weeping sores freckled his face like a weird *Mad Magazine* cover. Teeth big and white as Chiclets. Hair weepy and greased. The boy wore an embroidered T-shirt with *Princess* in blue cursive glitter. At the bottom of the screen was a tiny flashing name, "Jimmy—Jimmy—Jimmy", flickering like a ticker tape. He coughed up more stuff and flipped a limp wrist. Said to no one and anyone but mostly God: "Why am I dying here, alone here in this lonely room by myself? Alone because I have AIDS. *AIDS*. My blood is black. Dear God, help." For God so loved the world that he gave his only son, and he who believeth in him shall not perish (BELIEVETH—YES—AMEN BROTHER) but have everlasting life.

At that point, Jimmy took a bible off the bedside stand and threw it against the wall.

Fade to black.

Fade to death.

I couldn't stop watching from my cushioned cluster fuck. I felt chain-linked back in time. Surely, they will play a Nike commercial or broadcast the Coke wars. Give me a break!

NO.

It's like I'm back there. Watching. Living the death of this show.

The camera zooms in on Chandelier's face. So clean and shaven. He acts perplexed and sad, but his eyes are smiling. The voice booms from the surround sound speakers something about burning cities and Sodom and Gomorrah something-something-something. The TV got watery, as if to remember.

A retrospective of Jimmy's life.

Dancing with a pretty blonde boy, on a silvery strip pole in glowing glass bead earrings. Penis bumping penis. Ass to ass. Now kissing the lips of a gilded middle-aged man. Now mouthing the tent of the sheet. Now on velvet sheets eating grapes.

Boom... boom... boom. A voice. A heavenly herald.

Suddenly a trumpet blares and Jimmy sits up with bulging neck and eyes. He is still dying. Now alone and his wraith boyfriends turn back into demons. The green hospital room glows red as flames lick at his hips and fingers. He twists as his skin crinkles.

I wonder how Dad is doing. I bet he sends money to this place.

Chandelier looks out and warns the audience that this is not for the weak hearted. The electronic drums play upbeat music and the fat preacher is curiously flushed. I'm not sure, but I think he has a hard-on for the Jimmy actor kid.

The choir sings a familiar song: "*Onward Christian soldiers, marching as to war...*"

An orange number blip-blips on the screen as fake flames burn behind the digits.

TAPE 3
SIDE B

Evangelical Leader Dismissed Amid Sex Scandal. Haggard [Pastor of a 14,000 member evangelical church] told reporters he bought meth but never used it; he said he received a massage from Jones after being referred to him by a Denver Hotel. "We all have to move forward now," she [congregation member] said. "This doesn't make what Ted accomplished here any less. The further up you are, the more you are a target for Satan."

—Kim Nguyen, AP News
as posted on AOL News
November 5, 2006

Testing. Testing. Hallo. Dr. Jones?

Are you listening to this story?

It is 1-800-658-2548. I spell out the attached letters. 1-800-658-CLIT. Weird.

I'm sitting up now and I've eaten three peanut butter pickle sandwiches. I miss the fifth grade.

So there I was, dialing the number, which rang three times. A chirpy salesgirl voice: "Jesus loves you! Hello there, how can I assist your donation?" I didn't say anything because I was so mad and unprepared for such a quick pickup line. I hung up the phone and burrowed under the cushions with just my head out. I froze there for a few minutes, forcing myself to laugh deep down in my belly until it became a real bellow.

This is funny, right? This story? This thing I'm telling myself to tell you. It has to be funny or I'll wallow around writing maudlin hate-god-hate-parents-hate-life poetry for days.

I hit redial on the speakerphone. Another voice—still girlish—"Heeloo?"

"Jesus, Jesus, JEEEZZZEES!"

"Pardon me?"

"Jerry Garcia rules."

"There's no Jerry here. He quit three weeks ago, but I can put you down for a hundred dollars? You'll get a free Bible cover with zippered pockets for pens and a donation umbrella!" While she read her sales card, I hummed "Sugar Magnolia". Even the crazies are potential sales.

"Fifty will get you a year's subscription to *Right to Heavenly Life*, our monthly political journal."

Every word went up in a question.

"Ummm, and you will still be a lifetime member."

"What's your name?

"Julie."

"Julie, honey, will you marry me, or at least go out for a dance?"

"But you're a girl!"

The line went dead. The TV screen rolled on.

Chandelier is back on cue as he turns on well-heeled toes and walks with the cameraman into the next room. He explains that there are now six hell houses in the south and according to the money meter he now has enough to start building several up east.

Groovy Tuesday!

Now it fades to a girl strapped to a table. Garish doctors and a bone-skinny nurse come towards her knees with monstrous butcher knives, as if she is a side of beef. She leans back beneath the sheet and spreads her legs. The vampire-looking doctor disappears beneath her hospital gown, which has gone from green to spotted bloody.

He holds a clumped baby, which mews like a kitten. The nurse hacks the umbilical cord with shearing scissors. The baby doll goes blue-limp in his hands. A metal trash can lid pops open and the baby lies cold and naked at the bottom.

The girl hands a wad of cash to a cashier as she limps into the arms of her motorcycle boyfriend. They kiss.

"I love you Misty."

"I love you too."

Next, the scene flashes to a crinkling girl. A demon swoops across the stage taunting her name. Misty is burning in hell as her skin melts into different formations of face. It looks as if they have mashed brown silly putty over her nose and eyebrows.

I wonder how they got the mask to stick.

I used to press putty on the Sunday funny paper. It came in yellow plastic eggs. You could roll it flat to pull up the mirror image of Dagwood.

Above Misty, just slightly out of reach, a healthy pink baby floats in Winnie the Pooh PJs. It's a boy. An angel baby floating just out of Misty's reach. She burns and screams, "Forgive me... My baby... Me... Give me my baaaaby!"

A presidential voice booms murderer-murderer. As the Darth Vader type voice speaks, matching words flash on the bottom of the screen along with the 800 number.

I call the number back. This time a Cindy answers. I tell her I'm six months pregnant and about to abort. I ask if I can take the baby there so I don't go to hell.

Cindy puts me on hold. A rock and roll version of "Jesus Loves the Little Children" plays as I wait. *"Red and yellow, black and white, they are precious in his sight. Jesus loves the little children of the world."*

A man comes on the line. He offers to pray with me and explains that this is just the donation hotline. They do not take (cough-cough) babies here. I explain that I have been raped and this baby is eating me alive but I don't want to burn like Misty on the TV.

He puts me on hold. I've been waiting about ten minutes when the line disconnects.

The hour is over. Onstage, wattle man and Chandelier shake hands with clean-cut boys and girls. Rings glitter from their fingers and an American flag hangs beside the white and blue Christian flag.

Salute.

It would be easy to say these guys were on the post 9-11 flag bandwagon, but I have to tell you, they've been jingoistic for years.

Jingoism is a word I learned in college along with postmodernism, autonomy, genre, and intuit. I used these words a lot during freshman year. Sometimes in the same sentence: "So yes, I write anti-jingoistic poetry about the postmodern angst of the lack of autonomy; from this I intuit that misery is my favorite genre."

TAPE 4
SIDE A

Gannon University has once again been ranked by U.S. News and World Report *as a top-tier University in their annual edition of America's Best Colleges. We are also one of the schools awarded the distinction of "Great School, Great Price."*
—Gannon University recruitment letter
November 2006

I remember feeling smart at University, as if I wasn't a hick from Shade Gap, PA.
Ratty hair and Bible head.
Venison.
The stuff I tried to remove with the big words in a pseudo-intelligent mixture of stew I knew nothing of but used to make Mom feel dumb at Christmas and Thanksgiving.
Those four words, the exact location of Saturn, and the metric tonnage of Jupiter are all I remember from undergrad studies. $28,000 a year for six basic facts and they never even taught me to spell.
They say those who can't spell exhibit signs of genius, but as Grandma Sue always said, "'They said' is always the beginning of a lie."
I got a full scholarship so I stayed. My 38Ds mixed with test tubes and the fact that a hick girl got some money was enough to make me unlikable. Unpopular. Unacceptable. I did what I had to do; I drank my way into their hearts.
So despite being top of my class and figuring out how to dissect bumblebee brains, I became most legendary for my tequila consumption.
One Saturday during midterms, I had my maddest tequila drunk. I was halfway through a bottle of Cuervo Gold when I got the idea to do a body shot off of the crusty owner. This guy hated me because one time I ordered a drink he didn't

know. I told him how to make the drink, which he did, and then he said that I was a drink snob.

What bartender doesn't know how to make a bohemian butt-fucker?

His name was Em, which was short for Emmitt, and he wore the same wing-stained clothes every day. Green or brown polyester pants with a checkered cotton shirt. He was a miserable ex-military guy with a penchant for hating just about everyone except for white boy jocks and blonde girls. He was short, which only made him hate us more for spending our money and gawking around his 100-capacity bar as if we owned the world. There were even rumors that he was the head of the local KKK group, but no one's sure about that.

Quarter drafts and dollar vodka tonics amend many sins.

So anyway, it was fall semester. It was chilly and I felt nippy bitchy so I salted this guy's neck, threw back a shot and sucked on his sweat. There was a taste of skin grease and sagging balls, but I stuck to it until Gib handed me a lemon wedge.

Em's knees were shaking. The bar was packed and the science boys were screaming me on and on. So I ran back to kiss him on his oxygen starved mouth.

Dead on.

His spit made my lips and tongue taste like the floor of a city bus with grit and old smoke. At that point, I had to do something drastic or puke, so I did a swan dive onto the middle of a pool game. I rolled onto my back and swooped my arms in the arc of a snow angel. Then I cartwheeled into the side of the jukebox, which was playing Duran Duran. I stood up and gave a crooked salute. "Here's to the bourgeoisie!" Cheers! Cheers all around!

The bar was packed with kids who had just learned the meaning of this word, so the place erupted with stomps and claps.

Oh, the energy of the *newVo* intelligentsia.

Em was so excited that he bought the bar a round on the house, which was unheard of. Two hundred shots of tequila and then whiskey on my count of three. There's nothing like free booze if you're looking for instant friends.

A termite walks into the bar. What's he say? Where's the bartender. Get it? Where is the bar tender...
If you tell this joke to a PhD, they won't get it. Tell it to a first grader and they get it right away.

That reminds me of a scene from my life as a bartender-slash-scientist:

"Hi, what can I get you?"

"A Bud and you on the side, honey."

"That's a dollar seventy-five."

"You married, sweetie?"

"What?"

"Looks like you work out, with those arms of yours."

"What?"

"Got any kids?"

"Can I get you anything else?"

"What's your name?"

"Pick one."

"Hey, aren't you supposed to be telling me jokes? Tell me a joke. How 'bout a smile for Johnnie?"

"What?"

"OK, well, here you go, I'll tell you one, sugar."

"Nope. Listen, every time some drunk tells me a joke about buffalo cum or sticky cheeks, I want to come across the bar with a broken bottle."

"Yeah, yeah. Hey, you hear the one about turtles and blondes?"

"Fuck."

"The difference? The difference between them. If you get them on their backs, they're both fucked."

"Um, I'm blonde."

"OK, OK, how 'bout this—a fag walks into a bar—"

"My best friend is gay".

"OK, OK... Well, this Jewish guy and this Polish guy and a horse —"

"Hey, I'm half of both of those."

"—walk into a Catholic church... Hail Mary, he says... says to this nigger."

"Get outta here. Take your money. Out."

"Hey, I'm a Vietnam vet. You can't throw me out. I fought for this goddamned country. For this bar."

"Git!"

"Jesus, you're tough. Hey, is there anyplace fun around here? Place where I can tell my jokes?"

"Hey, listen. Here, take these peanuts on the house. And thanks for all that shooting you did. Hi, what can I get you? House special?"

"Sex with the Captain" 1/2 shot spice rum, 1 shot peach schnapps, cranberry, pineapple, OJ, shake on ice

—Memories Sports Bar and Café
Huntingdon, PA
1994

In case you're wondering, I continue to watch Chandelier every day at five because I lost the remote. It seems to have wandered off of the couch, so I'm stuck with god. Day in. Day out.

If you could see me, Doctor, you would diagnose this day as a massive panic attack. I try to close my eyes, but all I see then is my heart pumping and squishing blood through the chambers like Jell-O coming through fist knuckles.

Reminds me of the heart I saw on my grandmother's wall when I was six. I was sleeping in the room at the top of the stairs. It was the one with the horse-n-buggy wallpaper and the walk-in cedar closet. It was like sleeping in trees on an antique sleigh bed. I was underneath the quilt breathing to get warm when I felt this bumping. Peeked one eye over the cupped edge.

There on the wall was an oval bronze painting of a heart. There was a bracelet of thorns crisscrossed diagonally with plump tears of blood. It reminded me of the deer hearts Dad used to boil every December to make giblet gravy.

Well, ever since then I can see that artistic rendition in-side my chest, which is probably one of the reasons why I can't get up. Or won't. I mean, I guess it's a compulsion or a choice, depending on the day we're talking about.

Mom stares at me when I tell her it's a silent form of pro-test. But that's what I've been sticking to lately because it's hipper than an obsessive compulsion with my heart.

I hereby protest the purchase of society.

I even gave her this poem I wrote before I took off my shoes. Thinking maybe she'd get it. Get me somehow. Maybe understand. But no.

I cannot exorcise the TV gods. I hold my breath like a toddler. Maybe if I turn tantrum blue, someone will come to rescue me. I move nothing but my toes. I close my eyes and waggle the pinkie until I feel like I am walking.

I Sit 'n Spin my life into my naked feet. I need more toys.

I call Derek and ask him to pick up some LEGOs and one of those plastic spiral tunnels. He brings them by after a week of lobbying for the silicone industry. We crawl in the tunnel during reruns of *M*A*S*H*. We giggle and eat Cali-fornia rolls as Klinger tries to run in an apron and heels.

TAPE 6
SIDE A

Oh, you don't always die from tobacco. Sometimes they just snip out your tongue.
—from the singing Cowboy commercial
Truth.com
November 2006

I'm breathing easy, transfixed in the movement of my lungs as I shrivel them with blue smoke.

OK, so picture that film we saw in 9th grade health class. Remember those innocent lungs? Plumped and pink like a newly sewn pillow. Seamless. Then in comes this putrid smoke and the tissue folds into itself and the waving amoebae lobe hairs become thin cinder.

The camera flashes to a group of hooting teenagers in bellbottoms and insane hair.

The big daddy voice on the film says, "Jane and John think they're having fun, but they are slowly dying inside. Think before you smoke." Credits roll. Healthy kids stomp out cigarettes and snub those who smoke.

That was the day we all went to Morningstar's Corner Store to buy our first packs. After that, we went there nearly every day to buy Red Hot Dollars and Marlboro Reds. The cheerleaders bought white filter 100s because they were more sophisticated.

Smoking there by the silo, we had shag cuts and hip-huggers. Some of us went home later to milk cows or mow the cemetery grass, but for a few moments, we felt cool and urbane as if we were juking in New York City.

Seems like another life. Another me. I wonder what happened to the gang. Most of us quit after we got caught and grounded.

Some cut their hair off and got real jobs.

Mark got killed when his pickup tipped over.

Mike smashed into an oak tree the night before Labor Day.

Terry went under the wheels of a train.

Kipper did herself with a belt in the closet.

Some of us got fucked up and stayed that way for a long time.

I kept my white girl frizzed out 'fro and had a two-packs-a-day habit by seventeen. It was a relief to become addicted to something of my choice and I had the funny feeling that I was actually controlling my fate by choosing cancer.

As if I could thumb my nose at the Gods. Shiva, Jesus Christ, Venus, Plato, Buddha, Jerry Falwell, Joseph Smith, Bob Jones, Gloria Steinem.

Dying young seemed like the only way to be pure. That's what we all thought after Mike smashed his pickup into the oak tree on Airport Road just below the landing strip. Otherwise, how does a dead sixteen make sense? *"Only the good die young."* Billy Joel song.

That was the last funeral I ever attended, and I told Mom she'd better burn me.

"Never. Never lay me out like that, bloated with chemicals and made up grey. Spark me into the clouds or water." She will do what she wants, which will be to put me in a box with brass handles.

Vox populi says that youth feel immortal. That is why we didn't wear seatbelts and jumped from cliffs into shallow water. No. It's more of a vulgar gesture towards death. A silent fuck you—take me now—or never—kind of energy that made us drive too fast. Racing along the precipice.

It was life before cubicles. It was something. Things felt sharper. I don't know. Bigger. Edgier.

And then.

Sleep and work to pay for Saturday's sushi and martini. The great Disney Adventure. Foraging in supermalls in white Range four-wheel-drive Rovers.

Gotcha.

The perfect white shirt.

Crisp.

Shit.

TAPE 7
SIDE B

Spectacular views of the Corona del Mar harbor are visible from the huge windows in the bedrooms. And all the beds are made with 600-thread count linen Frette sheets.

—as reported in *Star Magazine*
November 13, 2006

I wonder what you look like.
I've hired an engineer from McManamon and Hecht to help me design a monster sectional couch, which I've pretty much drawn out myself already. I want an expert opinion.

I've designed eight segments, which will be arranged and hooked together to form a complete circle. Each section will be covered in brilliant colors. No white or black. Purple-cashmere-orange-cotton-silver-flannel-gold-burlap-blue-leather-fuscha-plastic-pashmina-yellow.

Yesterday I named the couch Kennedy Lane.

She will have all sorts of roll-out fixtures and a built-in desk for my computers and phone. I've even figured out a way to work out with a collapsible treadmill and weight bench. Both will fold up to slide underneath the platform end of the couch so neatly you won't even know they're there. Thank goodness for the age of little things.

The couch is about five feet off the ground so I can store more vintage shoes that I order from eBay every Friday. It'll have built-in file cabinets and drawers for my poetry and clothes. I'll fill the built-in bar with Shiraz and scotch. Everything will be set up on remote so I can open and close things without moving if it's one of those days. Finally, a king-sized bed will sit above the couch on a loft. The bed will be encased in a pine cupboard with out-swinging doors that can be locked only from the inside. Inside the bed are rows of shelves.

The entire platform will revolve on steel poles, which will be attached to roller wheels similar to those library ladders that attach high on a rail so you can roll around reaching for the obscure books. The wheels will hook to a metal track along the bottom of the couch so I am able to rotate the bed to view the rows of books I'll suspend from the ceiling in see-through Plexiglas boxes.

I've always wanted to swim through a room full of books.

I have everything from Plato and Jane Eyre to Stanislaw Lem and Stephen King. At last count, I had about two thousand books. The bookshelves are already in place. I just can't get to them at the moment, which makes me crazy. I order and read about fifteen books a week from Amazon. They know what I like. So I do that. Read what the cookies recommend.

The shelves go around a vertical track. The best way to explain is to describe a gristmill wheel or a dry cleaners rack going up and down. Nothing is alphabetical. They are in order of first read to most recently read.

Peter the Lonesome Hermit by Dorothea J. Snow.

Geek Love by Katherine Dunn.

Sexing the Cherry by Jeanette Winterson.

The floor is covered in stacks.

I haven't actually touched wood in years.

I can walk out of here; I just don't want to. I could quit smoking. I just don't want to.

The dust of my life is drifting beyond the safety fence.

I avoid the floor. I don't pee for twenty-four hours at a time. The risk of tripping on the way to the shitter is overwhelming.

It's exactly twenty steps to the cushioned bridge, eleven steps up and then five down the loveseat hall—four right to the shower. The problem is that if I make a mistake and walk twenty then eleven-five-two or any other incorrect assortment, then I have to turn around and re-step the whole thing.

One Christmas I fucked up because it took me six hours to get it exactly right and by the time I showered, I was wiped out so I lay on the couch and watched Jimmy Stewart's movie instead of phoning the kids or Mom. I get like that. Like I want to believe in old men angels. *It's a Wonderful Life. It's a Wonderful Life. It's a Wonderful Life. It's a Wonderful Life.*

After that, Mom brought over her fantastic pumpkin pie, half a ham, oyster stuffing, two pots of mashed potatoes, a stick of butter, and a Monopoly set.

I thought I wasn't hungry, but I wound up stuffing myself.

I ate everything and wound up playing the boat against the dog for three days. The dog, which I nicknamed Puppa, owned everything but the railroads and Baltic.

I like to pee and shower at the same time. I saw somewhere on TV that this process removes foot fungus. There was that time in the '80s when we all did it because someone said they heard Madonna did it. So we all wore crucifixes, bangles, and pissed on our feet.

After my shower, I rush back to the couch to burrow under my cashmere fringe throw. I love the wet smell of my citrus body wash and rinse.

I bought three cases on New Year's Eve for fun. We had that party at Clay's studio the night before the world was supposed to end but never did. I guess I didn't believe all the hype. Not really. But I wanted to because there's that lovely sense of no worries because what's the point? If the world's going to explode in a few hours, no one's going to give a shit that women are sucking off donkeys and men are sticking gerbils up their asses. Do your own thing.

The whole frenzied mess reminded me of Hurricane Agnes in '72. There was a flood, which gave the rain a biblical feel, so Mom saw it as an end of times sign.

The Susquehanna flooded the Governor's mansion and all those rich lawyers and that abortion clinic (especially the clinic) on Front Street were covered in stinking fish mud. It was six feet high and smelled like toe jam and death and everyone thought maybe Jimmy Hoffa would rise out of the mud, fisted hand to sky, as if to give meaning to divine destruction.

I think that's right. Things get weirded up date-wise since I've been here. Anyway, whatever, I just remember that it felt like everything we knew was about to be over.

Oh, that's driving me nuts. When was the Hoffa thing? I think he disappeared after Nixon made those tapes, which we never heard until the '90s (saying nigger and fuck and all that behind your grandma's back). Meanwhile, we're out there thinking *Thank Jesus this guy is a real good man. Morality and family values and all that shit.* At least that's how he looked, with the Checkers doggy speech and the pictures of his pigtailed daughters.

Anyway, we roasted marshmallows and skipped school for the entire flood week. I think Mom really thought we were going to float up to heaven with all the dead disciples. She was always talking about this trumpet going off then dead skeletons growing back pink skin on the way up to Jesus. She said that was it. The flood was a sign that was the beginning of the end. The end of the beginning. An explosion of glory.

So it was pretty disappointing when Monday rolled around and we were still eating leftover beans on toast and we had to go back to school.

It was funny, actually, because Mom had to lie to the principal and say we had chicken pox. That's why we were absent. But then the next week we both really did get the pox right after we played freeze-tag underneath the monkey bars with Jake and Chuckie Martin.

The doctor said she'd never heard of a kid getting the pox twice in a row like that.

No shit. Really? Well, no shit. You'd think someone who lied for a hobby coulda come up with something better than that.

By then, Mom was good and sick of kids in her hair, but Dr. Esther said she was to keep us home. So week two was spent scratching balls, ass, hair and necks, which drove Mom crazy. *Just be still*, she'd say on the way out the door. But we couldn't stop moving. It was hot. She had this idea that heaping quilts on us would hatch the pox quicker, so we were sweaty and miserable with skin bubbles. It made me think of hell or what it might be like as I lay there hatching stories in my head and blisters on my thighs. Hell, damn it to hell.

Shortly after that, there was the independent trucker strike. Dad had to ride shotgun just to deliver steel from Pittsburgh to New England. Every time he pulled out of the drive in his white Mack truck with the silver bulldog hood ornament, we'd cry our guts out because Mom would wave a hankie and say, "You may never see your father again. Lord willing." And then the little half smirk.

I half think she wanted him to get nailed so she could collect on the John Hancock life insurance policy for $5000, which was enough to buy a brand new Plymouth Barracuda. Plotting death by prayer proxy.

Around that same time, there was a bunch of dead cats turning up all over Fisherville. Mom thought for sure it was a satanic cult thing like the one in Jonestown. She figured it was a test from god to see if we could resist evil. So she stopped praying Dad would die in the crossfire of angry truckers. She stopped because she couldn't get the images of piled up bodies out of her head. She said they sparkled because of the dew and the spit on their chins.

As it turned out, the cats hadn't committed mass suicide. It was old Roy-Roy, who lived in the yellow shingle house on Sunflower Street. Apparently, the cats were all pissing on his prize *American Beauty* roses, so he put out pots of cream that he had laced with rat poison.

TAPE 8
SIDE A

"The establishment was still very much the establishment."
—Nigel Weymouth

Where did we leave off? Yes. Cats. My calico Claus was the first to go. I found him paws to sky, tongue hanging sideways. I'll never forget that week. The water. The mother. The reversal of fortunes.

It's cyclical. The sick. Circular. Comes on me and then back around. I can't help but chase my tail. I chew until the fur is gone.

So, having been through all those apocalyptic endings, pretty much nothing seems to end yet always seems to be on the verge of doing so. Like you are dying but never quite purple. Barely breathing with maybe one lung. Sort of useless on the one hand but extremely important on the other.

Like the retired condo-commandos in Wal-Mart stores bitching over the price of toilet tissue and denture cream. Hemorrhoid pads. Buy one get one free. Coupons based on epic films starring Charlton Heston.

Or the Crack Daddies and Mommies downtown with rotted teeth and sixteen babies in foster homes. Never see the kids except for Sunday visitation.

Or the Yuppie Daddies and Mommies working all the week long. Big screen TVs. Shag carpet. Expensive daycare. Two hours of quality time on Sundays.

Daniella-Josiah-Jamie-Johnathons livin' in a cardboard box. Living in a split-level. Settle them down with Ritalin. It's all the same, depending on how you look at it.

TAPE 8
SIDE B

"A hand on your cock is more moral and more fun than a finger on the trigger."

—Lawrence Lipton

Did you know the President wrote a poem? It rhymes. We were bombing Iraq but CNN wanted me to know that we had a writer in office, as if that would make him seem human. They don't know anything about poets.

God, I gotta fix this air conditioning. Everything feels so lukewarm. I want to be hot. I want to freeze.

TAPE 9
SIDE A

"I can't wait for this city to rot. I can't wait to see weeds growing through empty streets."
                    —Jean Genet to William Burroughs in Chicago
                                                    August 1968

I spent the last night out of my condo with TJ and Thomas T. Thomas. We went halves on a QVC special. It was a great deal—$700 bucks for millennium Bed Bath and Beyond products. It was all stuff you could use in case the electric stayed off due to Y2K. Everything was packed in foil and came with chewable vitamins so you could fight off free radicals and crazed city folks all at the same time.

The first twenty callers got packets of gourmet pasta and sun-dried vine tomatoes. I know I was drunk because I'd never cook even if Armageddon was going down, but TJ kept saying it was a bargain so we called in twice and actually got on-air with Susanna. She's the popular blonde. Anyway, TJ got so excited by the sound of his voice on national TV that he ordered six sets because then we'd get a forty-piece knife kit.

I remember sitting there pissed at TJ for using my MasterCard and he stood up on the back of an empty Rolling Rock case. "My New Year's resolution is to give up Godiva." Then Thomas T. Thomas jumps up and says, "I resolve to quit smoking and lose ten pounds." Then he mooned us. His pink cheeks were shaved and moisturized. I'm not sure, and I think this is a weird thing to remember, but I think he had bleached his asshole. I think if he could make his shit white and smell-free, he'd give a left nut.

I remember sitting there, hung-over and disgusted. Everyone was looking at my goldfish platforms. One of the heels had a crack that looked like a bluish vein. The fish, which I had named Parker, was dead because the water had drained out of the heel. One of her eyes was popped, as if I had slammed into something and jarred it loose. I took off the shoe and tipped her into the Tidy Bowl blue swirl. It was a sick moment of colors that didn't jive. I felt an unconnected clarity. It was immobilizing.

TJ kept motioning for me to speak, so I took off one shoe. I was standing there cockeyed and clear.

"I resolve to sit down on my couch and never get up. Please don't call."

Everyone sort of laughed and helped me gather up the rest of my sea salt blue corn chips and Scandinavian vodka.

I remember TJ shushing everyone.

I remember walking down the steps and home with one shoe off, one shoe on.

I remember sleeping for days.

I don't remember giving notice.

Two weeks later, the six cases of bath goods were delivered. I set up a website called Re-Gifters, which sold unused and unwanted Christmas, Father's, Grandparent's, Secretary's and Mother's Day gifts.

It turned out to generate about $5 million a year because no one wants shit gifts of blenders and ties. I pay 20% of the market value; they get cash for a night of happy hour fun. Resell at half the market value and I don't have to get off my ass.

I am paying a lobbyist to get some more useless holidays on the calendar. Currently in the works are Laptop Day, PC Day, and Auntie's Day. I expect to see these holidays wrapped into the back end of some highway or war-spending package.

TAPE 10
SIDE A

"Life in this society is, at best, an utter bore..."
—The SCUM Manifesto begins.

I'm scared, Dr. Bob. Lately, I don't feel safe. Sometimes, at night, my heart stops thumping. I swear it does. I think I'll die.. I burrow into my cushions. I plump the pillows so I have a teepee of sorts.

It seems like Mom always visits on my dying days. She gets so mad about my mental decompensation. I'm removed from everything normal and slotted. I don't live a calendar life, and this drives her crazy.

"You always miss my birthday! That's rude." She reaches over to straighten the pillows at the ends.

Usually, she won't stay long, maybe twenty minutes. On Wednesday nights, she stops by before spinning class. She likes to be shapely for Dad so he can fit her waist in his hands. I doubt she's ever had an orgasm.

I wonder why she always brings ham loaf. What the fuck is ham loaf, and who eats that shit?

I'm vegetarian. Every week I tell her: "Mom, I'm strictly lacto. Jesus, Mom. Jesus." Then she gets pissed because I take the Lord's name in vain. But she keeps bringing the ham loaf with blood gravy with those cheesy boxed au gratin potatoes.

She cooks everything up at her house because she can't bear to be busy while I'm sitting. She says she can't stand the way everything in my life is patched together like the clothes hanging on the projects clotheslines. She can't stand the way I have no measuring cups or tablespoons and just the one frying pan.

So she drives the food over to serve on a TV tray with a glass of water and two capsules of St. John's Wort, which she thinks will clear up my so-called depression.

She still makes me feel zitty and adolescent.

Retroactive.

She turns me into an illness.

Something that can't be cured.

She makes me itchy like mumps, measles, and chicken pox scabbed on one patch of skin. I try to fix myself by sucking on a cherry flavored stethoscope. An herbal mix won't heal this mental tumor.

Every week, she slides a black King James Bible under my TV Guide as if I won't see it. Every week, I mail it back to her house, certified. C.O.D.

"Why can't you be normal?" she asks. And asks. And asks.

She always brings up Penn Street, where I used to eat Buffalo wings with the other college kids. *Why don't you go there anymore?*

As if I miss those days.

No. Yes. No.

But I sure do miss the all-you-can-eat buffet at Hoss's Steak and Seafood on Route 22. The one we always went to after Sunday school. I miss the big fat booths and the three kinds of pudding. Butterscotch, vanilla, and strawberry. I miss the Sunday crowd. The big-tithing-non-tipping Christians. Mostly I miss the soft serve machine that pooped out ice cream.

TAPE 10
SIDE B

"With Acid there was an emergence of young people who dressed to die for."

—Christopher Gibbs

E very day, I think of food. I'm getting too skinny. Never thought I'd say that.

I look like a two-hundred-year-old Warhol soup can painting. I'm the one in the middle. Soup is soup. This is the best I'll ever be. A tin can painting with a manufactured label. Red and white. Rips scratched into the label.

Bought and paid for by AmEx.

Silk screens.

I remember when I bought my first Warhol. That was during my psychedelic phase. All of us trying so hard to be unique. Making stacks of magazines into toilets. Writing words on diapers and calling it "Book". Smearing bear shit over pictures of the Pope and Elvis and calling it "symbiotic erotica". Fashioning magazines from noodles. Forgetting how to read.

LSD.

MTV.

DSL.

iPod.

Crouching in a blood-red corner, screaming at pumpkins. Dying at the bottom of a dumpster with the other club kids.

Those were the days.

I should've sold those prints. Original Warhols are fucking depressing. This is it? Junk as art? Snapshots of snapshots? Paint me a fucking picture!

TAPE 11
SIDE A

"How long did it take you to grow your hair that long, Danny?"
Rifkin smiled. "We always figured that if we ever held a press con-
ference, the first reporter to ask a stupid question would get a cream
pie in the face, and you're him."

—a Grateful Dead press conference

No, Dr. Jones. I can't give you my original Warhol.
Please don't ask again. Payment in cash only. Let's
keep this arrangement strictly under the table.

If I were out, I'd buy two suits. One blue 1968 vintage
boutique style with frills.

One black Donna Karan. Two suits to wear to bed to
cascade over the pillows I stuff between my legs to keep
from masturbating more than twice a day.

Two by two.

Noah's ark.

Starbucks and orgasms.

Toddlers and Volvos.

It is.

The way.

Things are.

Done done.

I even buy two cans of garbanzo beans every two weeks
from e-mart's vegg2u.com.

Everything has to be divided by twos. Last month, I had
the ceiling tiles removed because I stayed awake for six days
counting and recounting from corner to corner. Trying to
make things even by splitting atoms.

I kept coming up at odds.

TAPE 12
SIDE A

Breast Milk Martini: Baileys Irish Cream, Chambourd, dash of Hazelnut and Tequila Rose; shake-n-pour into martini glass.
—Heather Doyle's Golf and Country Club
Blue Knob, PA
1989

I keep remembering the bars. The whiskey sours. The way a daiquiri masquerades as a fruit smoothie.

Woozy guy at the Brass Rail Sports bar. Thinks he's gonna cheat on his wife with me. Thinks I'm impressed that he owns a contracting company that took him from skinny kid to overfed bowl of wobble. He is the consummate Santa. The big daddy come to save me from myself.

"Honey, you're as sweet as a box of Lucky Charms. Damn. Can I get that light beer, sweetie? Ummmhmmmm, I'd sure like to be that cold bottle between those titties of yours. Ummm, I'm in room 121 if you want to stop by after your shift."

A smile. It's easy to lead them on. Twitch the ass. Leather skirt hikes up. They place bets. A twenty says she's not wearing panties. I point to the winner. My tip jar fills. Is he actually slobbering? His golf buddies roam the bar drinking and tapping the floor with their pool sticks. A young one in a blond buzz cut sits quiet at the end drinking Coors Original. He wants to look but is too nice. I'll fuck him till his balls are blue.

Then and now.

Skinny and fat.

I'm losing it today. But that's what you're paid for—correct? To figure it out. Stay the fuck away from my soup picture.

I wonder if Gypsiemama is online. We met in a chat room for single parents about a year ago on a lonely Easter Sunday. Her kids were with their dad and I was experimenting. I went by the screen name Juris2000. I told her I was a lawyer named Arthur. I like talking to her, but lately she's been asking to see me. I don't have any shots to post because I burned all my fat pictures.

The only one I kept was of me in Cincinnati with Spot and Dave. I had on a purple high waist dress with white cable tights. My cowlick was lying straight and my bangs were smooth.

It was the year of kindergarten and I had cute little points of teeth and pink tongue. I was still charming. We were six years old in dresses or denim bib overalls; there are three photo albums full of cuteness. Before we got big. Ugly and big. Dave was pinching my arm in that shot but I was still smiling because the man behind the camera told me to.

After that, we got ice cream cones and mine melted down to my armpits because I was holding the cone up like the Statue of Liberty. I kept the grin.

I used to love ice cream, but lately all food feels like sand. I try to think in terms of white chocolate macadamia nut with salty-sweet butter pecan but come up with nothing but a gravely tongue.

It's like being back in the sixth grade. Puking up dinner like a wizened, cancered thing.

Thank god they didn't have a size zero then. Size 2 was bad enough. I remember lying awake, pounding my hipbones. I was proud to smile, despite the pains in my stomach and the clumps of hair on my pillow.

Here she is now. Online chatter.

Gypsiemama: how r u
Juris2000: fine n u?
Gypsiemama: grooV the kids r at schl I hv 2 hrs freedM I mssd u uday we awys tlk on tsdys whts up?
Juris2000: nthin M wrkin on a big case cant tlk lng I misd u 2 hows The protein diet? Lose nE ass? LOL LOL I becha u R so HOT Hey can we drop this abbreviated shit?? I feel like using real old-fashioned full-lettered English words. Would that be possible? I feel like a stupid teen when

```
I say U r nice. Sort of like I'm about to x or o
at the bottom of the paper, as if I can't really
read or something. You know?
Gypsiemama: well ok I guess but I thought is
kind of fun that way. Can we meet sometime soon?
You sound sort of sexy.
Juris2000: Well, no. I'm not well. GTG.
logoff
```

Did you catch all of that? What in the world is she thinking? *Sleepless in Seattle?* Every woman to see that movie now thinks she will meet her online *one.*

As if the Internet is a magical Cinderella place.

As if we are real.

As if it isn't just another form of the rubber doll.

Well, Dr. Jones, there are some fantastic porn sites, I can tell you that. I was going through this stage where all I could think of was pigtails, knee socks, and farm boys. Anyhow, I was looking up farm porn when I happened onto this site.

The front page had this blonde bending over with her pussy sticking out of a burlap bag. She had hooked a finger into the crotch of her panties and pulled them sideways into a soft stripe of pink.

OK so far.

I'm turned on.

I guess I should explain that I first had sex in a haymow.

It wasn't great, but it was young.

It makes me wet.

That and my Y2K shower gel.

Anyway, we could hear his dad calling the cows. Then calling us. Then sort of screaming. We nearly got caught. I had on pink Tuesday underwear. Bits of yellow straw were poking me in the ass and I bled all over it. It was a ripping thing, a sort of wailing thing, and then a dripping thing.

So now I think of farm sex on Tuesdays, because there's nothing to a Tuesday. Every other day of the week is something. Monday, first day back. Wednesday, hump day. Thursday, day before Friday, which is the header of the Saturday Sunday weekend. But Tuesday. Tuesday isn't much at all. It's a spacer. A blank day. By the time I was thirty-five, I had forty pairs of Tuesday underwear.

So on Tuesdays I search for farm sex sites. Farmsex.com. Point. Click on the bending blonde's finger and up pops a graphic of a man in cowboy boots and he's fucking... fucking... a fucking chicken. Up the ass. Wings. Beak. Claws. Chicken shit. All that mess.

My goodness.

That stuck in my head for weeks. I'd be sitting here knitting thigh-highs and up pops a chicken.

A car squawks in the lot. I see a robin pecking away at a worm. My mind twists. I can't get away from the thought.

Chicken.

Penis.

What's next? Men in scuba gear getting blowjobs from toothless sharks?

Women and skunks?

I know its phobic of me, but I can't walk out of here with all the green slime of humanity.

TAPE 13
SIDE B

All lines must form at section C. Sidesplitting emails. Now available wherever you are.

—Blackberry Pearl advertisement
November 2006

It's like layer upon layer of plaster of Paris mask face impressions.

Have you ever had a face impression?

Jones? Have you?

You lie there while the artist globs plaster over your cheekbones and eyes. You have a straw in your mouth. You breathe through the tunnel. If you aren't careful, the gook will drip into your lungs.

Note to self: don't use cracked straws.

Teensluts.com.

No chickens here.

I'm having difficulty staying on task. Saying what you need me to say. Saying things in a way for you to order them into your particular file system.

TAPE 14
SIDE A

Masturbating Mosquito: Sours, green apple schnapps, melon liquor. Shake over ice into a large glass.

—O'Malley's Beach Bar
Hollywood, Florida

"H*i, can I help you?"*
"Gin martini, dry with a twist of lime. Not a hunk of lime but a twist. Do you know how to do a twist? You have to peel off the meat and twist merely the rind. It's the essence. The oil, if you will."

"Everyone's a bartender. I suppose you know how to make a cosmopolitan? How 'bout a surfer on acid? Russian Quaalude? Masturbating mosquito? No? NO!"

"Just the martini. Martinis. Dry. Very dry. Look, just tip the vermouth till I say so."

"When?"

"When."

"Say when. Now? Now?"

"Are you getting smart with me? What? This is awful. Where did you get these stale olives? Dump this and make another. Do you know who I am? Hey, lady? Do you? Know? WHO. I. AM? Where's the manager?"

"That's six bucks."

"Get me the MANAGER!"

"Me. That's me. Owner-manager-whatever. Me."

"Where's the bathroom?"

"I. DON'T. KNOW. I just work here."

You know this is voluntary, right? This sitting thing. I meant to do this. To be here, out of the chaos. Away from subways and gin bitchy women. I bet you think I'm lonely here and maybe that's why I talk to you, right? Is that what you're thinking? Actually, I talk because Mom is convinced I'm crazy. That and the money, which she wants. Which is what makes the world turn 'round. Which is why you listen to me.

I won't commit myself.

They'll build a new church with five tall steeples. Open the door—see all the peoples.

She expects you to straightjacket my arms down so she can watch me slobber through window mirrors. But you wouldn't get paid then, would you, Dr. Jones? Would you?

Tell you what. If you can get me off this couch, I'll give you a million dollars. Write me a letter that will get me back into lists and day-planners. Do that.

Yesterday, I counted my business planners. Most of them leather. Twenty-seven organizers. Each month-day-second-nanosecond-holiday-birthday-engagement-marriage-divorce-court-date, each and every one is plotted in jagged blue strokes.

Like a math graph.

Grids of days of interactions to be had.

Appointments to meet.

Check.

Catch 22 to read before midterms.

Check.

Spaghetti to cook by six.

Check.

Was that life?

Was that my living life?

I was normal then. I did my time. I didn't see the kids except for Saturdays after soccer and Sunday mornings before brunch. Children are so resilient. My generation read a book that said it was just as well to spend one good hour a week with the children instead of meals, baths, and everyday play.

Quality time became our hectic mantra because it was all we had.

They said what we wanted to hear. We heard what we wanted them to say. Our children call home for quality chats on holidays. We taught them well.

TAPE 14
SIDE B

Who says yesterday's news can't be tomorrow's too? Life's a Journey.
—Samsonite advertisement
November 2006

Here's what I want you to do. Write up this report for Mom. Say: "Hopelessly addicted to silence; patient is thinking herself to death."
Prescription: solitude.

It's weird—sometimes I feel like a brain that's been removed from the body and placed inside of a marmalade jar with purple Kool-Aid. I put the jar inside a nuke shelter. I swallowed the key. No one ever gets me. They don't.

Enclosed, find a check for $5000.00. File this tape under "the politics of money".

My engineered couch is coming in sections today. $20,000 later and it's only partially complete. The movers will be here around one, which is cool because I don't feel like working on my dissertation today.

I never really told you I was working on another useless PhD, did I? I'm researching the effects of sitcoms and movies on human sexuality.

Currently I can say that since the advent of TV we've been spending money on penis drugs, plastic surgery, ass reduction, and hair growth. In addition, we purchase vagina lubrication, rubber condoms, AIDS insurance and bath bubbles. The movies aren't much better, but they are bigger, prettier, and they have plots.

I blame Plato.

There is no perfection.

The idea of strangers in my space is tweaking me out. I'm degenerating. Maybe I should cancel. Should I cancel?

No. noNoONnNONONONNNNNOOOOOO!
Whee!

It's been so cramped living in the second-class section of this commuter flight place I call home. Like you can never deplane and there's a body beside you with cheap strong perfume. A mixture between ass and roses. Budussy (butt and pussy combo). You sneeze and choke and eat peanuts, and still your nose convulses.

You want to get off so badly and there is a wanting so weary that it takes over like a ventilator.

The need to wiggle or giggle during a sermon.

The need to piss on something wrong, like the face of a clown or a gavel.

Close a book.

Rip out a page.

Gag.

TAPE 15
SIDE A

Let the moment capture you. Destination PHX.

—escapetophx.com

It's been a strange week.
Some days I feel like that documentary I saw on live-CAM.

Mark was his name. He was this guy who sailed solo around the world. He started off somewhere in Maine. He was the executive type, handsome and bottle-tanned with a trim goatee. Just quit his job as CEO of some lumber company and bought a sailboat. Had a wife, two kids, a Doberman, and one hell of a midlife crisis. He was sponsored by Mawntawks Camping Equipment, Inc., J.C. Smathers and Sons, and Bluetail's Fishery. They covered his mortgage, supplies, and allowance for the kids. The local TV station agreed to air weekly footage as a promo for the nature channel.

At first, everything was beautiful and banal. He tuned the sails, read Frost, and waved to the kids, but after four months of sailing alone, Mark went bananas.

I think it was right around Christmas when he appeared live on the six o'clock news without eyebrows. Then he started making stretched out faces in close-ups, pulling his lips tight over his teeth like a horse licking peanut butter. It was so bad you could see his nose hairs.

The next thing you know, he's clipping his toenails and showing his sore feet. This was broadcast without edit.

To make matters worse, he was eating spaghetti. Gorgeous Mark took the noodle through his nose and down the back of his throat and out the mouth. He sort of sawed back and forth with the noodle. It was like elementary school all over again.

Ratings shot up, but the high-society wife was embarrassed.

She had connections.

That was the last liveCAM of Mark.

I liked Mark. He reminded me of the second grade with the white paste balls. Sometimes it's hard to tell the difference between boogers and gum.

The new couch is here. The moving company sent six men. They wear dark blue chino pants with stenciled T-shirts.

One has long sideburns, but he's young. His nametag says Mitch. He's looking at the map I drew—turning it side to side and in circles. I offer him a mug of Columbian brew before I take the paper and write North. South. East. West.

I tell him the gold velvet couch is North.

"Start here," I say. And I realize that I'm jilting my words, as if I've forgotten how to speak.

Mitch waves at the rest of the crew and they clop into my den with the silver sectional. After that, it starts to make sense as they fit the pieces together like a toy train track.

Mitch keeps saying, "Ma'am?" And I understand why because this place only makes sense to me.

But I wish he wouldn't do that. Look at me and say Ma'am like that. Like I'm fucking crazy or something. I have this urge to put my fingers on the nape of his neck and push until my thumbs tear the skin. I have the feeling that with the blink of my eye I could become a killer Ninja Witch Queen. And he would stop talking and calling me Ma'am.

He's tolerating me because I'm a big spender and they're a little company. I know this and that is of course why I want to kill him. I hate a person who can be bought so easily.

I am overwhelmed by the sheer number of these six men. The smell of skin and aftershave merge with the sound of nametag Steve burping, then muttering, "Excuse me." Walking in heavy work boots on the place where I bleed through box after box of tampons. Flush. Bleed. Flush.

I'm stuck here and fresh out of morphine. I don't have any pot. They expect me to talk or to motion or to walk on the floor as if I'm normal.
I need chemicals.
I need.
Sugar.
Something.
I'm standing here talking and they watch me through hazel eyes. Some are blue. One guy has green.
Mitch makes a cell phone call as the coffee gets cold.
This is bullshit. I am bullshit.
Lately I chant when I get nervous.
UmmmmBattahBattahUmmmmmBattahBattah. Which I do. And the chanting freaks them out, but I gotta hand it to them for working on through.

This reminds me of yoga class and the great self-pampering that occurred in the '80s when we thought Trump glut was uber cool. There was this sweaty yoga shop that Myra told me about. She said it was the best-kept secret of the in-crowd. So I went.

There was this earnest little man in a white diaper-looking-thing with his large muumuu wife. There were pictures of Buddha and a rock garden. Fish swam in a tropical tank. Paddle fans spun. Indian music tweedled through the speakers. I felt as though I had traveled to exotica.

It was 110 degrees in that place. They said the heat was a mirror of our flowing selves. Get in tune with your breath. Feeeeeel the movement of your spirit. Give yourself a hug. Yeah. Yeah. I know how to masturbate. Variations of stretching.

I felt sweat running down my ass crack, which was annoying, but after about ten minutes I started to relax into my private space. Sadly, this guy beside me started vocalizing his breath—hunnnnzz-hunnnnz-uh-hunnnnnzz. He was so loud. It broke my mood. So I looked over and there was this doughy man with baggy shorts. The thing was, well, I could see his balls, which struck me as funny. So I'm lying there cracking up, just busting out all over myself.

"What?" he says.

"Oh, for chrissake, put that shit away."

The man clamps his hands over his balls like they're priceless eggs and then slumps out of class. The yogi master guy then comes up to me and asks me to leave. He says he'll refund my money but please to leave—to please—to kindly leave—to please to not ever come back—please.

He was acting so peaceful and gentle, but I could see this vein punching a beat in his neck. Later, Myra told me that the ball man was his financial backer. So that was it for the yoga phase.

After that, I tried training for marathons, triathlons, and decathlons.

After a month of that, I got a shin splint. Dr. Morrissey said it was time to slow down.

Loiter.

Focus. Stay focused on the movers.

Mitch is still here. The sitting part is together, so now they're working on fitting the underneath things. Shelving, bathroom, big screen, and treadmill.

"I can see you listening to me babble into my tape, Mitch. So I'll tell you a story, if you hurry it up."

"OK," says Mitch. He patronizes, which I will ignore for now.

"Once upon a time, I met Plato. It was the year of purple paisley shirts and bell-shaped sleeves.

"I was studying cell dissection. It had something to do with replication and dissemination or the taking apart and putting back together of things. I enjoyed the Godness of cells—or lack thereof. The coldness of having to peer through metal to see a thing squirm or be sliced. And I was fine back then in my quiet lab coat with the neat white lapel. I was clean. Rubber-gloved and sterile. You could almost hear me squeaking down the hall like bleached tires on tile."

"Ah-huh," says Mitch as he slides the treadmill into place.

"It has to touch the couch," I say.

He nods. "Sure."

"So then I took this Greek class because they said I needed three humanities credits to graduate with a BS, so I signed up for 'Studies of Platonic Love' because it was the only class open on Tuesday/Thursday. I bought the books and amused myself with the titles, which I can't remember to tell you now. I don't know exactly, but they were mushy and hippy-like.

"Well, I expected to see a lot of longhairs soaked in patchouli. We science majors didn't take philosophy majors too seriously. It was as if they spent their days finger painting cursive ovals onto tissue paper. They talked of air and spirit. This major required drugs.

"My world was of the real. Blood, skin, genetics, numbers. Skeins of chemicals and scales. A tapering of blood beat into my veins. My science. I had this lust for chilled freezing things and stainless steel. Plastic goggles. Things that could be figured and plotted or graphed. There was no hypothesis for gods or love, and I liked it that way.

"Two plus two?" I ask this to see if Mitch is paying attention because I need for him to do that. To listen.

His eyebrows go up and beam a silent "Fuck you, lady."

I'm beginning to like him.

"Mitch—can I call you Mitch? Or is it Mister something?"

"Mitch is fine."

"Well, Mitch, there shouldn't be cracks at the connecting points. It has to be this smooth circle. Take a look at this drawing. See here, how it hooks at the bottom?"

"Finish your story, lady."

"What happened to 'Ma'am'?"

"What?"

"You know, when you got here and you were calling me 'Ma'am'. And I hated that."

"You told me to stop. Don't you remember?"

"Well. No. Apparently not." I'm beyond trying to impress. I just want to talk to something other than the tape recorder.

"So I walk into this class expecting to ace everything. I was so superior. In fact, I expected to learn nothing. Before class, I joked with Jon over in the science quad about mail-order PhDs.

"I walk in and there is Dr. Wagoner diagramming an isosceles triangle. It was perfectly angled. This was fifth grade stuff. It was strange to discuss points of lines in philosophy, but at least it wasn't hippy-goddess-love crap, I thought."

Mitch interjects, "Yeah, I hate that, too. Love beads, my ass."

"So you know what I'm sayin'!"

He nods and nails something to the floor.

"Very cool. Anyway, Professor Wagoner looked at me and pre-med Marty Janik and said, 'Today, we will discuss Plato's ideas of the really real. Do you think a triangle is real? Is it perfect? Is a circle never-ending?' And so the class began and I was sucked in by the philosophy of numbers and then the story of Aristophanes.

"Androgyny and love have always fascinated me. Mitch?"

"Me too."

"You missed a screw."

He nods. I go on.

"OK, so here's the deal—there's this story of the third human being or the first or something like that. According to this Greek guy, there once were these round creatures with four hands, feet, legs, and ears. They had two sets of sexual organs and just one head with two faces. The theory goes that they were so completely happy that they didn't need the gods, therefore they began an ascension towards heaven in an attempt to obtain the ultimate purity."

"The heavenly orgasm?" Mitch is great at multi-tasking. I'm in love with this man.

"This pissed off Zeus because he had a dick and was a dick. Naturally, he wanted to punish them but not kill them because they were, after all, pretty amusing. So he sat there on his square throne and thought about what to do... what to do. Mitch, can you guess what he does?"

"No."

"No? Well, he slices the creatures in half in a weird kind of sexual amputation. I guess it was sort of like pulling a cookie apart with the cream on just one half so then the other half tastes just dry."

Mitch reaches into his lunchbox, which is sitting by the door. He doesn't say a word. Just hands me an Oreo.

All I can say at this point is "Wow." He gets it.

"These creatures felt unfit and empty. They were so sad without themselves, or what they thought to be self. And this was Aristophanes' explanation for lovers and falling in love. We can never be complete without our other half.

"So these human things spent their lives in a state of schizophrenia. To fix this vacuous loss of self, they began hooking up with everyone in sight, which was fun at first but then became misery. Sometimes they stuck with one person so they could be happy until death.

"Don't quote me on this. I'm great at re-writing history. But it is my take on one-night stands and marriage and the parts I can remember about that philosophy class. Maybe we can't help ourselves. You know what I'm saying?"

"Yes, Ma'am."

"Shit."

"Lady? What do you want me to call you?"

I ignore him because I'm on a riff. I can't stop.

"The problem was that if pieces didn't fit, then the two had to split apart, and more would be missing. Sometimes an arm, a leg, or a head would fall off. Often it was hard to tell where one person began and the other ended, but they kept on smooching up with other halves because of the friction and because it felt better to try. Being alone felt wrong. After all, what good is half of anything?

"Mitch, at the very least, can you please get the purple and orange sections completed today? I'd really like to sleep there tonight."

TAPE 15
SIDE B

Rhinocretaire Desk designed by Francois-Xavier Lalanne; price available upon request.

—jgmgalerie.com

Mitch is gone. But I'm still talking.

So anyway, all of this made sense to me. I remember when Tiff got married and moved to Denver because she couldn't... just couldn't... could not... live without Travis. He was beating her bloody and fucking her bowlegged, yet she stayed.

"My other half," she said.

He always bought her roses afterwards and then a Mercedes and a house in the Whitebridge gated community.

Then she gave him a daughter. A finely woven replica of herself.

The kitchen was lined with copper and Italian tile. She cooked faux pas with pate and fine saltines.

When the baby shimmered with the mirth of the terrible twos, my sister fell down the steps and died against the antique sauerkraut crock from SonShine's Antique Boutique on Magazine Street.

Instantly. Poof to ashes.

She's beside the Boston fern in the purple vase. Silken dust. A small bit of fine bone powder.

So I've seen the effects of the "I can't live without you" thing. I have.

It's a spearing, gutting death that begins so seamlessly with the waggle of an index finger. It is a grind that rotates the hip pins, so wet and smooth that you can't feel the pinprick drip of spinal fluid. You think Mother-Mary-Joseph! I just had four orgasms in one hour... This one's a keeper. You don't notice the slice right on down to the soles of the feet.

The tender arches that are necessary for walking.

67

The toes you can no longer curl.
Cowboy boots can't splint broken ankles.
Hindsight really pisses me off. What's the point?

TAPE 16
SIDE A

"When I started Screw, *the government didn't like what I was doing. Fuck the government. If we're not allowed to own our dicks and our pussies... we're not in a free country."*
—Al Goldstein, editor of *Screw* magazine

He's here again.
"Mitch, can you hand me that hammer? Some penny nails. A Phillips head screwdriver. Any tool will do."

I hammer and talk.

"So anyhow, back then I really bought into the story of Aristophanes and the idea of my missing better half. It made sense because I had been slicing off bits of myself since the eighth grade.

"First there was Ted—he kept a pinkie finger. Then Stevie. Michael. Michelle. Jody. Melanie. Freeda. Daniel. Georgie. Ginger. Sara. Russell. Rosalie. Heather and Derick, with whom I inadvertently, purposely had sex in or on or got fucked by until there was nothing left but the stump of me."

Fuckers and fuckees. All the way through high school. We played soccer, drank our milk, took our vitamins, and massed on Sundays.

"Do you go to church, Mitch? Is that too personal?"
"Easter."

"With Aristophanes' succulent grapes in my head, I began to have dreams of me flipping through the air like a quarter at midfield. Dallas Cowboys. That's who I liked."

"49ers." He nails with an ear tilted towards me.

"Heads-tails-tail-tails-tails-heads. The silver lining never seems to land, just spin. Wait and wait for the thud, for the settling into mud. But nothing.

"I remember feeling like maybe I had hundreds of halves. Millions. I couldn't find the center molecule. The place of beginning. What people call heart. Nucleus.

"I began to search in earnest. I hung brown butcher paper on my bedroom wall. I painted in what my grandma told me I was. The thing she drew with charcoal. A tawny twelve-year-old body with Band-Aid knees, buck teeth, and pooched belly. The me I was before I forgot how to skip rope and crash toboggans into snow walls."

He nods. And nails.

"I markered off sections I knew I had lost, in red acrylic dots, which I numbered. It started out like an orange with ten neat membranes in veined segments beneath the eye sockets and around the lips. Then near the bottom by the shag carpet, flush with the big toe, things went crazy. Shooting up and into the hips, the dots became clotty and layered around down and under like a salty blood pomegranate.

"I worked on that project for weeks. Months. I'd come back from physics class with a cold coffee and just stare. Stare at the window cracking out into millions of trails leaking in every direction. My body hung on the wall upside down.

"Sutured. Ruptured. Sewn back anew.

"I started eating the button eyes from my rag doll collection. I could feel them plastic and cold against my guts as cotton poofed out of my ears. My friends stopped coming to the dorm because the eyeless dolls freaked them out and I was never hungry.

"I began to find embedded cartilage and bone from my lovers as they rose to the surface like porcupine quills. I became unrecognizable beneath the mustachioed bristles.

"Have you ever felt smothered, Mitch?"

"One time I got stuck in an elevator. Is that what you mean?"

"Shit. It's OK. How much do I owe you, and will you be back tomorrow?"

"Well, yeah, there's that last sectional to screw in."

He's gone now. And I remember.

I remember sitting on a corduroy couch with Geoff. Blond Geoff. I looked down at my torn daisy jeans and thought, 'This is it. I've got just this knee and that thigh and then I will vanish in an unspectacular burp of air.'

So for the first time ever, we ate something other than me. Does that make sense? We had rare porterhouse steak and shiitake mushrooms in butter sauce.

I didn't even kiss that boy. But we chewed and laughed and talked about the latest Burt Reynolds movie and how his jeans were so tight in the crotch that it looked like he was split.

Afterwards, we ordered a fudge sundae, which we melted and stirred into chocolate cherry rivers.

And I felt affection for that freaked-out hair and those wild blue eyes. He had the look of something skittish, as if he were about to leap from a cliff at any moment. Like maybe he would rather gnaw his knuckles just to feel the movement of his jaws. It was like he belonged in a steel Sahara as a modern day John the Baptist, all hairy and drunk on honey bee juice. He'd be the one to rip down cactuses and drink the prickly blood from his wounds.

No, wait. Better yet, a number in a Russian novel.

A rebellious 27.

Plucking eyeballs from robots.

Starting revolutions.

And later generations would say "Wow" and think 'What a god—what a man.'

And he knew that I knew. That I craved him. That I was starving. That the sexual revolution didn't mean a damn if I couldn't have his soul.

And I knew that he knew. And I knew that he couldn't run fast enough or dive beneath my wanting. And so he vanished as if he were air and I had made him up in my wet dreams.

And his gone-ness made the wanting more.

Made me want to put him in a suitcase or rope him down to a steer.

Made me want to murder like Manson.

Hating myself for not seeing it coming. His going.

And wishing I had slicked my eyeballs to the nape of his neck or sewn my bottom lip into the slipknot of his beard.

I've been chewing myself since then and there is nothing left but clear candy wax lips on a stick.

If only I had left something on him. He may have called. May have looked in the mirror and seen that part of me hanging off his shoulders. Mailed it back.

I had to drink him away and now my liver is half-gone and he is back in my head.

To tell you the truth, I didn't remember him until this past April when I was reading the back of a cardboard matzo ball soup mix. Crazy to make soup on a camp stove. I crouched on the futon section and stirred and read. Sugar, salt, monosodium glutamate, spices, annatto color, Geoff, cottonseed oil, garlic. Add egg and shortening. Stir. Form into balls. Geoff.

I stopped right there and did a shot of John Powers.

He was my flatfish cartwheel.

"I missed talkin' to you."

"Thanks, I guess." Mitch has lost some of his suck-up-ed-ness.

I feel lonely. And I don't understand it. I'm down to begging. "Stay till four. Take this hundred-dollar tip. I'm not nuts. Don't say anything. That's OK. Go on home, drink a beer, watch a sitcom, laugh with the track. Scream at the red-lights."

He takes the tip but doesn't stay.

TAPE 17
SIDE A

Turn a few heads. Weave your own spell. Euphoria eau de parfum spray. Euphoria Blossom eau de toilette spray.

—www.dillards.com

They're gone now, but I can still smell the citrus cologne. It reminds me of that mix I invented. At the time, I was working for the government. Good money. Full dental. Retirement plan. Twenty-five personal days. Blue Cross and Blue Shield.

It was my first real job and I was fresh out of grad school. Up till then, I had been bartending at clubs and local dives, so I was anxious for solid hours and stability. One minute I was pouring redheaded sluts into shot glasses, the next I'm mixing green chemicals in glass beakers. It sort of felt the same, although I did get to wear a neat lab coat at the new job. And there were those twenty-five days off a year.

I put my hooker boots in storage and gave my leather miniskirt to the Salvation Army.

Things change. Things stay the same.

Your neck droops. You get smoker's cough. You buy new underwear. And yet. And yet there you are, stirring things as always. Mashing aspirin with wooden pestles. Buying fresh oregano on Tuesdays. Dressing in cuffed beige on beige. I couldn't really feel anything other than a silent wearing away. A smoothing of corners. A disappearance around the eyes and lips.

I began to pencil in my features. Some mornings, I'd forget makeup and my lab partner Gib would ask me if I forgot something or if I was feeling OK. I began to keep eyeliner in my holster.

I was the team chemist in the B division. Section 228 at the Rockaway Naval Base in Connecticut. Most people have never heard of the place. I'm sure you haven't. There were four groups of fifteen people. We worked from six to six in gray and yellow brick buildings.

We didn't know what we were doing. Not really. But most of us had big student loans, so we didn't ask questions.

At first, they gave us paperclip work. Filing. Checking stat reports.

Then they asked us to keep secrets.

The hiding places of nuclear waste.

The real cost of gasoline.

The cures for cancer.

Those who were silent got moved to level C with a 20% pay raise. They gave us a project. It was top secret and something to do with sterilization. They asked us to develop these chewable pills. After that, we worked on a translucent patch. It was covert, but we didn't know why until Gib started dating that brunette lieutenant.

Marcenca was her name. They were fuck buddies for a couple of weeks and she wound up telling him that the pills were going to be handed out to career welfare moms. They planned to give the pills and patches to new mothers as a new trial postpartum anti-depressant. The recipients would sign waivers and receive $200. They would be required to wear the patch for one month with check-in times every Monday. At the end of the month, they would get the money, some vitamins, and vanishing ovaries.

Marcenca said the feds figured to save $10 billion within the first five years. Each clump of baby was worth about $30,000 in saved food stamp funds per year. Take that amount times tens of thousands of kids, and you've got enough money to start wars in Bosnia, Israel, and Pakistan. Excess funds would also be diverted to American farm subsidies. Dumping excess milk and rotting fields of wheat takes time. Money.

Gib was pretty upset. He was a hippie who got into science because the psychedelic cell shapes reminded him of shrooms. He was brilliant. Anyway, he wasn't sure who to tell, so we met over lager drafts at Ellie Mae's for happy hour. He told me all about "the plan" as we did shots and talked about Nazi motherfuckers.

While we were sitting there, Marci was strangled with a Fitness 2000 jump rope, the one with the gold weighted handles.

We saw the undercover cops outside of Gib's apartment talking to two guys from upstairs. Not a good thing.

I took Gib to the bus stop and gave him all my cash. It felt like *Starsky and Hutch* or *Hawaii Five-O*. In fact, I kept expecting someone to yell, "Cut!" But turns out it was real.

While we were riding to the bus, Gib wrote out his will and as much of the story as he could fit on a bar napkin. He told me to get his guitar, Grateful Dead records, and Ferlinghetti poetry. He said, "Mail it all to Mom." I remember holding the napkin in the rain.

I remember running in my red spikes. I remember tripping into a mud puddle and then a curb.

I never heard back from Gib. He's either dead or still hiding. It has been twenty-some years. I imagine he's dancing on a street in Mexico. High. Tie-died.

I call his Mom on Mother's Day. She always cries. I could use a Mom like that.

Believe it or not, I didn't quit that job right away, which kills me. Fucking Jetta payments.

But I did start slacking because of what they did to Gib. It wasn't what you'd call anarchy or subversion because they did have a great dental plan. No, it was more of a malaise of that general government-type meander through days of abnormal cell structures. It was the beginning of purposeful mediocrity.

Still, I felt guilty for being there without Gib. I felt like I owed his mother something. Every day, I thought of how he smelled that night. A mixture of sex and essence of tangerine. I couldn't get it out of my head. It was opposites attracting. Like buttered nylons and ground patchouli.

Intoxicating to be in love with a dead man.

I wanted to bottle that smell so I could wear Gib on my sleeve. So I started messing around with scents. I knew it must be hormonal. Feral. Like the deer musk dad used to spray on his hunting overalls but better. Nicer. How could they not smell the black powder death behind the musk?

I figured humans were about the same and there were plenty of ugly people who'd be willing to spend twenty bucks on a piece of possible ass.

After a couple of weeks, I came up with a unisex perfume. Initially, I tried to market the stuff to department stores, but I couldn't get past the snotty receptionists. I was about to give up when I flew to Miami Beach for a long weekend over the Fourth of July. I was drinking in a leather bar when I met the owner of a midsized cosmetics company. He said I smelled like sex. I sold him the rights to the perfume. We wrote out the agreement on the back of a napkin, which I didn't lose in the rain.

We called it *X*, the scent of the beautiful people. There were black and white glossy ads—mostly skinny sexless couples with bee-stung lips. Obscure messages went below the pictures.

Pink Kandy.
Out... Julie.
Intrinsic Fence.

Everyone pretended to know what they meant. The ads ran for several years. I hated them, but I made 30% profits on sales. I put the money in an account for Gib's mom. It's still there. She says Gib can have it when he comes back. She says it like she knows he will. I wish I had faith.

I started flying to Miami every couple of weeks to dance and pick up my checks. One day I met Sandy, a city cop. She always carried a gun and a walkie-talkie. She made me feel safe. We went to Isle Mirada to make love and drink rum-runners. Eventually I quit my job to be a bisexual, which was in vogue. Still is, I hear.

It's funny how a smell brings it all back. It was just now that I smelled the perfume on Mitch that I thought of Gib and Sandy.

Funny how that works. Forgetting, blocking, and remembering whole chunks of my life as if they aren't real.

And then today I see online that birth rates have declined by some forty percent in the inner cities. Congress is apparently excited about the surplus money.

Pork chops for dinnah!

I'm about to make my nightly run to the bathroom. My skin is crawling with sawdust. I always drink too much sangria. The couch isn't together, and it is driving me mad. It's crooked together like a train wreck at odd angles.

Maybe if I do the roly-poly, things will be all right. I'll hold my ankles and roll in no direction. Rock side to side. Round and back and forth. Then finally down so hard that I pop back up like a Weeble. Heave and roll and zigzag across the floor. Close my eyes, smashing away and screaming. I can actually see the blood creeping across my eyelids like grasshopper legs.

Two more steps to the door. Four to the toilet. 2-4-6-8, who do we eliminate?

I'm in. Stripped naked. Soapstone white like ivory. I will erase this tape. Soon I'll shower beneath the bed. I will peel African mud facials from my cheekbones to be beautiful again. I foam with the round cake of soap.

TAPE 18
SIDE A

Enter the ageless future. Perfectionist correcting serum for lines/wrinkles.

—Estée Lauder

Can I look yet? Open. OPen. Owepen teh dorr. My IQ is drooling into the puddle outside my window.

I've been standing in this shower so long that the water is January. I'm talking to you naked. My skin is raspberry and pimpled into sandpaper. I've been on my knees in the tub. Has it been hours? Moments? Days. My fingers tiptoe over to the back of the toilet seat. Where is the towel... the damned towel? Itsis sisits sits it sits on the floor. K. Open the door. K. Turn the knob. Kay. Hop... hop... hop. The seat, the lap, the couch. My gold velvet couch.

I guess it's easy to assume that I'm having panic attacks, but I'm not really scared. I'm not fucked up. I just have different brain waves. Think of Tick and Tock rocking the same pendulum.

This has been happening since the fifth grade, back when they had no name but bad for what I was. Teachers thought I was lazy or faking sick. Once I slicked myself to the mirror in the boys' bathroom from noon until dismissal. I couldn't stop staring at the urinals. I actually had this urge to eat the blue piss cakes. And I knew that would make me sick, which is what Tock said. Tick said lick, lick, lick, bite. Incapacitation occurs when there is swinging inside my head like that.

Mrs. Swailes, the typing teacher, got me by slamming the door with a wooden paddle that was shaped like a fat boat oar. There were holes drilled in the ends to cut down on the air drag. I'm sure I didn't cry. I was grounded to my room for six weeks, which is where I met Annie.

I'd double your shrink salary if you could help me get back to Annie. Her peppermint skin is fading. Her fizzy black hair is a sketch on my wall. I can only imagine. I read and reread my journals.

September, 1976. It still felt like summer. The room was white hot lonely with bed, desk, and bible. The wasps were building paper nests on my window. I spent hours with my ear to the buzzing pane. Ladybugs crawled on my fingertips. I cut a hole beneath my bed to hide chocolates and comic books. Through my window, I could see the backside of Fisherville's cemetery and baseball field.

Days alone in my room. Days and days. Meals on trays. Door closed. Light bulb burnt out.

I started dreaming day and night. I met her after midnight. My great-aunt Annie. She was the one Pap never talked about. The prostitute. That's what they said about her because she brought the railroad workers home during the Depression. She always had money to feed her baby brother.

The family was ashamed, but they didn't want to starve.

I met her in a speakeasy. It was 1920 and I was wearing patchy bib overalls and brown work boots. I felt as if I'd been there before. Annie walked up. More like a slide up. Hip to hip, she hitched her bare toes under the wood bar rail. She leaned into me. So close, I could see her eyes glowing. Something between hazel and green. Egyptian cat eyes, corners slanted and winking like a slow golden backwater.

She sucked me in slow.

I couldn't look away or wiggle out of her grasp.

A bitty butterfly wing—weak and wet. Stuck in her amber veins. Locked up. Chained down. Glued at the brow. Prisoner. Statue of me sitting. Falling into her eyes.

She pivots to the bartender and orders a root beer for me, a straight scotch for her. Rolls a cigarette. Bits of tobacco snow to her knees. She bites a piece off of her lip. She inhales and her hair corks upward and out of its twist. A blue haze dangled in hookah circles from the corner of her lips, oak soaked in wine. Our bubble was languid with soda and sway.

I felt a tweak of energy just beneath my skin as if fingers hovered just above my arm hairs. Tickling the nerve endings with spirit ripples. A finger traced my cheek with strong skin. A warm voice in my earlobe. Somewhere, a translucent membrane began to throb.

"Where you been all my life, baby dahl?" Shiver baby words. Neck crinkling murmurs. Demanding breath. I wanted to be inside her belly, striated with fur and tongue.

Spinning on my barstool, I turn and turn until it pops off the pole. My knees are stuck full of peanut shells. Bleeding chin dimples into a wail. Annie bends down, but she doesn't bandage the wound. She licks it like a Siamese cat. Tips the blood into the corner of her mouth and cures me with strawberry cream spit. My face is full of numb tingles. I don't move. Can't move. Stretch my heart around her neck.

A trail of square tiles sneaks around a corner. I grab a map.

The next morning I wake with the quilt so twisted that I can't move. I have to roll off the bed to the floor, where I unravel the knot I've made.

I try to sort things, but my head is tangled and braided. Last night's macaroni is pebbled to the plastic plate. My fingers skate from nape to toe. It's all me. I cannot name this thing I felt. Feel.

Inside.

Grounded.

I became a kept woman.

I sat by the window for days and days, watching the wasps and twisting my hair into wet sops. Matted and bruised, I chewed the windowsill. Splinters stuck from my lips like quills.

I wasn't hungry, which was weird because I lived for food. Constantly. Vanilla ice cream, steak, burgers, peas, corn, and jelly bread.

Chomping.

Meaning.

I guess I knew something was wrong when I couldn't stomach Wednesday dinner. Egg noodles and salmon. I saw the food crawling on the tray in symmetrical doodles. Noodled A-B-Cs and fish bones leered with seer eyes. I forked.

Missed. Pasta skittered down my shirt. Clammy brown snarling things sucked across my skin. I skipped the plate onto the tin roof, where the pieces pelted the grass.

Skinny. Skinny. Too skinny. My anklebones and wrists became jutting fragments, which I clicked against my hips. Tapdance. Annie, Annie, where have you gone? I am eating myself alive to feed on your bones. And then she came to me in the dark sleep to fatten me with iron pan cornbread and buttered snap-peas. She knelt by my bed and whispered stories of willow angels, cave bison, silver rivers, grapevine cabins, and candy cane wind vanes.

Camped beneath my mattress in plumes of fire. Milked nipples laced with camphor colostrums to keep me alive.

I miss Annie.

TAPE 19
SIDE A

Chewing hard foods, such as apples, toast, raw carrots, and new cabbage, gives your jaws plenty of exercise. And you are breaking your food up into little pieces so that it will be digested more easily. Get the habit of chewing all food well before swallowing it. Remember to keep your mouth closed when you chew. You do not look nice when you chew with your mouth open.

—Growing Big and Strong
1939

Where did I put that horseshoe hammer? Ball peen hammer will do. Sledge hammer. Tomahawk hammer. Root word: ham.

I want a Lebanon bologna sandwich.

Some try to remember birth. I am a tunnel rat. Each day burrowing in towards death. Digging barehanded. Closer. A little bit closer.

You can feel death alive. Did you know that? Are you for real?

Stop button. Stop. Erase. Rewind. Fast Forward.

Here's what you do. You lie back. Close your eyes. Feel the scalpel slicing through the delicate onion tissue we call heart. Bump. Electric shots bleep zags to the balls of eyes. So quiet it's deafening. You hear germs speaking of love and war. Bones disintegrating. Ants carving rice. Sarcoma splitting—playing doubles.

Some try death sex. I keep to closets. Couches. I won't choke an orgasm. That is for rookies.

Forget.

Deadlines. Sixteen-hour days.

Escape.

Giggle. Hang upside down on your flowered armchairs. Cackle in the back of your throat.

Become airless and weak.

Look back, way back, in the corner of the base.
That blue pulse that jumps the rope.
The place of weeping.
Of twitchless lips.
Thawing tongues of honey.
Crack up.
There are no computers here. No news is good news.

War blondes. President? Mr. President? Where will we land our next coup? How many children will you bomb or feed and on what day and when will that be? How is your lovely wife? Thirty million at the box office. Ratings are... ratings are good. Polls are up. She's great. Reading to white kids in libraries. D.C. sniper hits again. News. Any news? Same news? Every day. No news is good news.

Crawl on back to the speechless stuffing.
Get into your own head.
Everyone else is wrong.
You are right.
Keep telling yourself that.
Isn't that the definition of crazy? Not thinking like others. Swinging on monkey bars. *She can't think her way out of a paper bag.*

Have you been to the circus? Those motorcycle acrobats go round and round in metal ball cages. They can't stop too soon. Too soon to stop, to die, to fall from the roof of the cage. The carbon monoxide fumes lazily. There's more than one way to kill a cat.

I doubt I'll sleep well tonight. I feel amorphous and blobby. Lately, I haven't been exercising. My skin is turning doughy.

I have to email these invoices. CapsLock. Enter. Delete. NumberLock. Fuck. Why is everything so conveniently inefficient? I got logged off right in the middle of Wesson, Beth for $29.95. She ordered four packs of nylons, two CDs, and a pencil set. Bills need paid, checks must clear, statements need to balance.

Stocks. Bonds. Dividends.
Add to cart. Add to wish list.

Lately, I sleep during the day for a few hours. I'd rather be alive in the dark. *This* seems to make more sense at night.
This sitting thing.
No one will stop with casseroles or magazines.
I burn nag champa.
Chew the ashes.

TAPE 20
SIDE A

Household hint #866: A sure test for a down pillow is to hold the center in the palm of your hand. If the corners sag, get a new one because the down is worn out and you're headed for nothing but insomnia.

I've been rearranging my sleep schedule like I once did for the babies, but in reverse order. We were up at 3 a.m. with mechanical breast milk or formula so I could sleep while he fed them. Forcing nature into neat 10-to-6 schedules to match our careers.

Then you blocked out feedings. We began to bond in increments.

After that, we stopped having sex because we smelled like sour milk. We pretended to be farmers with our metal carts, shopping for organic carrots and peas. Only the best for you and yours. We swam through fortified peanut butter and La Leche League meetings. We worked so hard to raise them right. You purchased the Volvo station wagon. I bought the Beethoven tapes to play during naptime. Baby genius or die trying.

Originally, we didn't mind. We thought the pace would ease up and we'd get back into our selfish fucking. But days went by without any sign of a penis or tongue. Then years of...

Preschool, soccer, T-ball, ballet, and swimming. Varsity. Varsity. Varsity. College. College. College. The goal is.

We became bespectacled librarians. Clicking and cataloguing times of days and hours into slender walnut boxes with brass handles. We skewed ourselves into an impossible playbook.

Yet again. And again.
Fumble.

I with my butter knife, you with your boot. We were fighting something just in front of the closet.

Interception.

I'd fought this battle before.

Off-sides.

I introduced myself.

Instant replay.

"Hi? It's me. Hello? What, who, you, yes. Oh, yes, certainly."

There is a certain familiarity.

A shootout.

"I met you in... Wait, wait, don't say it. Boston. Yes. In a bar in Boston. We had sex and then two children."

Score.

"Victoria and Nicholas," you echo into a green longneck.

"Yes. Oh, and you are the mother."

Slide tackle.

"Dear god. We should do this more often."

Quarterback sack.

"How are you?"

Foul.

"Wait."

"I'm mad about something, I know I am, but what is on the tip of my tongue?"

Halftime.

"How've you been?"

"Do I know you?"

Substitution.

"Didn't we fuck?"

"Used to. Every day?"

Game.

"Called it 'making love.' Said 'love.' Kissed. Eight years ago. You remember?"

Set.

"In the T-top Trans Am? In the gold post bed? The room with all the mirrors? Pool tables? Washing machines?"

Red card.

"If I recall?"

"Sort of."

"Sort of impaled on each other. Before the infants."

Overtime.

"I remember now."

"Yes, it was so good that I stopped writing that science fiction novel and you stopped doing whatever it was that you did back then and we were inside each other three, maybe five times a day. We slept a lot."

A lineman is down.

"Ordered in Chinese or made fried pierogies. Sometimes I'd make eggs Benedict with the cream sauce and we'd drink leftover merlot or vodka, depending upon where we were. Mostly my place because you never had coffee."

Always thirsty and craving sugar. But we didn't care and for a while there, for that bit of time, we stuffed the hollow parts with tissue and our echo became like a dormant toothache.

Forgot to mold clay.

Forgot to tumble words and form plots.

Forgot to pay the phone and the electric.

Forgot to weed the grass. Ate straw.

The dishes disintegrated.

We sucked till the marrow was gone with no money for transplant.

Then you got fired for absence and I deleted my 400-page report on cell mutation.

No deliveries.

I thought maybe we should call it quits. We should have but didn't.

I tried, that day. It was sunny in January and I tried to walk out but I forgot my own name.

Well, John, he's down in his rookie year. Sad. So sad. Yes, Brent, he gets the 1999 Drumstick Award for courage. Well, John, he's paralyzed, so he'll need it. See you next Sunday. Back to you, Terry.

I needed your skin-coat. I found it lying by the bathtub, warm and sleek. I crawled into you and felt delicious. And you thought I was devoted because I was *so into you.*

People said we were cute. Sickening in love.

89

We played. Without the plastic spinner and dice. Bought property. Paid taxes.

No one ever seemed to win.

Pass Go. Pass Go. Go to Jail. Pay $200. Pass Go.

Things began to melt around the irises and backs of hands. It was a slow searing.

Dumb frogs.

Swim in boiled oil.

Cheesy as a fat beach romance novel. No plot. Chapter one: fucking. Chapters two and three: same, but in different places. Chapter four: all same. Chapters five, six and seven: restaurant dinners, diapers, dinners, TV dinners, breakfast. Chapters eight, nine and ten: kinky meatless skeletons. Nerveless convulsions. Ropey thighs and knees.

Should have hit it on Route 66. The last impossible jump. Too much for even Evel Freakin' Knievel.

One day I was running my fingers through your hair and my nails got tangled in your braid. It was like a Chinese finger trap puzzle; the harder I pulled, the stucker I got.

The children.

I felt dazed. Whacked out on something. Dizzy. Like I lost the how to manual. Maybe never saw it in the first place.

They kept calling me Mommy.

Initially, they cried a lot.

I bought Spock and Chicken Soup.

For six months, Nicholas screamed. Screamed so hard his belly button popped out.

Herniated.

I pulled open a trash bag. I wanted to dispose of the noise. No mother would ever admit this, but we feel it. We do. That precise moment when you can no longer breathe and your man's gone hunting. You roll the baby out of the cave. Saber-toothed tigers are starving just below. But then, just then, you turn into another day. They smile. Grab your finger. A first tooth. Two giggles. Baby powder necks.

Night terrors.

You try to be a good wife. A good mom. So hard, you try.

You bury things.

Plant flowers.

Try to be wet.

But the roasts are overdone.

The meringue is not quite stiff enough. Spider webs abound. You eat too many chocolate chip cookies. You get a fat ass. He murmurs into your clavicle that maybe you should be sexier. Start step aerobics. If not, perhaps work. Get health insurance. Buy milk. Careers are nice. Accolades. You miss one too many soccer games. Forget the milk. Buy fast food. Turn on the TV. Miss open house. Can't remember snack day.

Fingernails gnawed to the bone.

I never got the socks white. Not once.

I took a class on blowjobs. How to give them. How to please a man. Keep your man. We used bananas or cucumbers. They made me gag.

Webster's dictionary: Felitio... How to spell this word? Fel... Fil... Fuck...

I don't know how to say the word. What is the word? How to say it nicely.

Suck cock!

Everything began to taste of leftover meatloaf. Freezer burned.

I don't know. I don't.

That's what I said when you pinned me down one day on the Sesame Street bunk bed. The kids were out back in the sandbox. The one we got for $49.95 at Toys"R"Us.

On sale.

Family day.

Shopping day.

Sunday.

Nicholas was digging tunnels with the gravy boat. Victoria was peeing in the moat. They used ketchup packets for the castle flags.

I don't think I can do this. That's what I said. You were trying to enter but I was dry as cracked pottery.

I felt unraveled then, as if there were no center. No ball of yarn. I felt as though I should begin the twining process of gathering myself together. In the shadow behind your head, I saw Rice Krispie treats and lottery tickets. I made up a haiku as I opened my legs.

It is possible to rape yourself.

Remember me? Me?

Who are you? That's what you said that day. The kids were singing row row row your boat gently down the stream, merrily, merrily, merrily, merrily, life is but a dream, and you forgot my name.

Mommy?

Wife?

We'd been going at it for two decades. We gave the sandbox to charity. Nicholas was at Notre Dame studying Russian poets or something. Victoria was studying for her SATs.

It was Sunday night after the playoffs and we hadn't seen each other for weeks and that's what you said.

I saw you standing there in that designer shirt. A variation of that same polo shirt I bought you every Christmas. I forgot your name but I recognized the shirt. $69.95 with a 5% increase every year. Macy's.

I don't know you anymore.

Thank god I had the receipt.

That's what you said.

No. But no.

But I have a shared file.

Inventory: twenty years, two washing machines, one Volvo, three VWs, a van, 936 bi-weekly paychecks deposited into a JOINT account, two retirement funds, a green riding mower, one in-ground pool, two MAs, one law degree, one PhD, double indemnity life insurance, 1040 brunches, fourteen shoeboxes of Kodak moments.

You taste like glue. Like ground bones.

But I have this paper. Black and white proof. Exhibit A. We were lovers.

Fiction.

Were.

Were not.

A fancy plot.
Were too.
Outlines.
Not.
B-movie.
Too.

Prove it, you said as you began to peel back the skin from my thighs as if I were a boiled tomato. The mush came off in slippery clumps.

I licked your arms. You tasted of someone else. My tongue felt as if it had been dipped in candle wax.

You used to taste of me. Of musk and wet.

I licked and licked at the wound until my tongue was raw and the ache reached the bottoms of my toes.

Beef stew was bubbling and the cornbread mix was black with flies. I told you they were raisins. We ate together. Slathered on the butter. I straddled your thighs and tried like hell to fit but it was like a cocktail of rosaries and marijuana bleach.

TAPE 20
SIDE B

Household Hint #859: If your bed sheets are wearing thin, here's how to give your bed coverings a brand new lease on life. Hold the sheet up to the light to see thin spots. Before the sheet actually begins to break, tear it down the center, sew the outer salvaged edges together and hem the sides. The portions along the selvages are stronger because they receive the least wear. Before sewing the selvage together, rip back the top and bottom two or three inches from the selvage. Then overlap the selvages and sew them in a flat seam. Resew the top and bottom hems. Hem the side edges to prevent fraying.

Opposites do not attract.
        Not in subdivisions or split-levels.
        Things fell apart.
I began to write drugged poetry.

    memories gut me from spleen to throat
    I should take more Polaroids
    tattoo the plastic border
    spring 1994
    grilled steak and bacon
    we were?
    i was?
    stave the wrist drip
    butterfly Band-Aids
    scatter the swordfish
    bloodied quilt patch
    darning blisters
    morphine Mercedes navigate me
    kaleidoscope jump rope
    miss mary mack mack mack
    all dressed in black
    my last lover?
    i can't recall his cheekbones

blonde maybe?
brunette?
halfway tall possibly short.
quantum theory?
elegant fingers inside me
lottery tickets
no money for bread
married twice?
what?
till death?
what?
legal letters
i graduated?
i did?
baccalaurei artium?
what the fuck does that mean?
saline mango roots
scribble meaning in the sand

I wrote that poem and it was weird how I started walking around like I was a verse. In a haze of spot rhyming maudlin.

I forgot who owned the kids or was responsible for tuition. Victoria would tap me on the shoulder: "Love you, Mom. Love you."

"Yes, yes, you too. I do, I swear."

"You forgot me at soccer again today. We had a game today. Remember, Mom? Try to remember, Mom."

I'd look up from the floor and there would be you and twenty messages on the answering machine. Things about games and court dates. Money that was due for electric and insurance.

I'd be sitting there with poetic piles of anything and everything from napkins to scribbled coffee filters.

The whine of my life.

Sometimes I wrote in crayon.

I took personal days.

I slept constantly or not at all in gluts of days or minutes.

One day I wrote over sixty-three poems. I ran out of paper and the computer had crashed so I scratched them into the marble countertop and the copper oven hood.

Penny nail pencils.

I felt purged.

Sanctified.

Clarified.

Then everyone got home from work and school. I looked up over my horn rim glasses and tried to explain the way things bubbled up over my eyes and how things seemed so blurred and wilted.

This isn't funny. That's what you said.

The counter cost $4000 to replace. Out of pocket expenses.

I missed her winning goal.

I couldn't help myself. I cried myself to sleep. I kept blacking out. Mentally backspacing.

I'd be sitting on the toilet or standing in a line and my lucidity would slip.

I'd wake up at the Colonial Park Mall. The country club golf course. Towne's hair salon. My closet office.

It was like I couldn't chew gum and walk at the same time.

I didn't expect Gregg to understand. But I thought he'd stay until I sorted things out. Give me some silence. Let me turn over the car payment and the season tickets. Just take a little break.

But he started packing things up. Ties and suits and the twenty-some polo shirts. His hips made my eyes water.

For several weeks, we knocked around the house bumping accidentally. Touching in spite of ourselves. I'd walk into the bedroom with a stack of towels or a pot of hazelnut coffee. He'd jump or trip. Sometimes clear his throat. He'd come to the fridge for a Pabst and I'd be stirring the dishwater. I'd cough. He'd snort. One of us would go to the bathroom. Lock the door.

It was a place beyond explanations. Black holes. Language barriers. Hamburger Helper and stilettos.

But the money was good.

We nickel and dimed ourselves into overextension.

Not worth a damn on paper.

The everything of our lives together was lumped in attics and closets.

Which is why the moving and packing was really getting to me.

There were so many things I couldn't find. Locating a spatula became Herculean. Finding the tweezers, impossible. *Where is that first set of towels we bought at Bon Ton? If that sonuvabitch took my punch bowl...*

I felt as if I were in a giant game of hide-n-seek. I was constantly looking in the forsythia branches or behind the tool shed for fry pans.

There were chunks missing from my memory.

Victoria would say, "Mom, remember that time you said you could jump the ramp on my skateboard and I said no way so then you flew sideways and broke your right knee? Remember it was so funny cuz that cute ER doctor said it was unusual for a forty-something mom to get pre-patella bursitis?"

And I'd think to myself, 'Not me. Wasn't me.' Because I didn't remember that year. Or the next.

But I knew she wasn't lying. And she knew I was losing it. So I'd laugh along with her as if I shared her memory. The wrinkles of my brain were impenetrable, crusted with too many insomniac grim reaper dates. I wore sunglasses at night like the song.

I was the producer of a shitty musical.

No director.

Coke wouldn't sponsor this show.

Gregg moved out.

He was experimenting in bisexuality.

Men named Ken and John-John called when the four o'clock bars closed. All I could think of was shit on Gregg's dick. We switched to the quilted four-ply paper.

After about six months, he seemed to recall his preference for bouncy tits so he hooked up with an eighteen-year-old named River. He'd found her painting murals down in the subway. He was so heroin happy. She was unique the way I always wanted to be, with rings in her eyebrows, black lipstick, and unwashed clothes. Now why didn't I think of that?

Everyone said he was being a bastard. And I hated to admit that I didn't want him anymore, it was just that he had left me. I wanted to leave him in a scorch of has been... I just wanted him to remember my exit when eating buttery English muffins from her pillow. Instead, I've got this dumped feeling.

He was more like a chameleon, shedding old lovers like inconvenient tails.

I'm more like a staggering oak tree, fat with rings. I strap lovers one atop the other like a giant snowball, sticking myself up with enough ice and granite to be called a boulder.

TAPE 21
SIDE A

Household hint #865: Linen is a fussy fabric, so beware ironing the creases in the same place in your napkins and tablecloths every time, for this causes breaks in the thread and wears out the linen.

It's Halloween. I turned on AMC, hoping to catch old Bronson or Fonda Westerns. Civilized murder.

Six guns.

Prostitutes.

Gangsters in trench coats.

Hangings.

I'm an immobile mobile; there's no breeze to move me.

I haven't slept for eight days. I used to think I was making a political statement by staying here, but really, I'm nothing more than a hermit of the year 2000-something. I'm a weirdo who lives up in my condo mountain eating grubs and canned garbanzo beans. There is no point of re-entry because I'll always be batty.

I'm fruity with flies, like a rotting July peach.

Out of sheer exhaustion, I stay on channel 29. They are running a *Halloween* marathon. I watch I, II, III, IV, and V. By 4 a.m. I have become intimate with Michael Myers and Jamie Lee Curtis. They are my screaming siblings. I never understood why these movies were so scary.

Preachers selling haunted hell house tickets, now that is scary.

Carpet mushrooms are scary.

I've always loved October, with the ghouls and orange sugars. I still order candy corns and pumpkins with my groceries every week. I like to put the corns under my lips like fangs.

Growling at myself consumes hours.

Witches and demons. I used to have parties. Gregg would cover the floor with cooked spaghetti. It was our house of brains and guts. When Victoria turned fourteen, she asked me to stop throwing noodles on the floor.

"Jeez, Mom, I'm not twelve anymore."

I ignored her.

By the mid-eighties, our yearly costume parties were huge. Adults love to pretend more than kids do.

Guys in drag.

Women in leather straps.

Me at the door in a Marilyn Monroe costume, all boobs and white film with a fan under my legs blowing the skirt up. I was wearing a strap-on penis that gouged out when I turned sideways. There were twenty rented black-and-white TVs whomping bad seventies porn into the air. Gregg smoked a pipe and wore velvet as if he were Hugh Hefner.

That was the year Mom and Dad broke the ten-year silence because I had given them grandkids, a new batch of babies to save.

Mom was dressed as Mary Magdalene. Dad as John the Baptist. I didn't tell her that Mary might have been a hooker. Their church was having an "alternative to Halloween" party where you could read verses and dress like your favorite bible character.

So there we were, me in drag, Gregg wrapped in Saran Wrap but otherwise completely naked. At that very moment, Brad walked up in a black and pink pantsuit with purple glitter. The plastic penis on my leg came unglued and Mom's headdress slipped sideways. Dad was already turning to leave Gregg's beer. I had an epiphany, just then, of our dysfunction. The possibilities were endless, the depths limitless of how much plumbing it might take to tap our disorders.

She gave me a letter. Mom was always writing letters of apology. Back before Dad died, she was sorry about everything. There was a fantastic aura of guilt, which she wore like a tiara.

"I'm sorry." She said this through her burka as they walked down the steps. I don't remember what she had done. Or why I should forgive.

I was piss drunk. I tried to read all six pages of her navel-gazing cursive.

I called her the next day. She asked if I understood what she was saying on page 3, which I'd used to light a smoke. I said yes.

It had taken her a day to write that apology. She tacked it to the door as her voice went up in martyr flames. It was enough to keep her gone. I didn't see her for a year, which was fine until they found the lymphoma in my neck and groin.

Then she came, waiting for me to die. It gave her a reason to exist: to minister.

Every day she came with broth and magazines. She drove me to every gut-ugly chemo treatment. In '79, they hadn't perfected the chemicals. I lost thirty-six pounds, which put me in a size four. I remember telling Mom that at least I'd die skinny. I bought leather pants and a butterfly string bikini. I loved the mirror. I'd lie on the couch sideways and stare into the tall reflection of bony me.

My slim euphoria didn't last long enough. After days and days of gagging and puking on every level of your split life, you begin to beg for death. You lie there and think of sharp knives and things that will splay veins or stomach linings. You throw up into buckets. Your eyes hemorrhage. You think maybe they're hanging by a thread but there they are, dry-wrenched into your skull.

You dream of dying like a dog on a soft pile of flannel rags and maple leaves in the back of a log house somewhere by the edge of a creek.

Then finally, one day, you get there. Half asleep, you paddle softly downstream. Your lungs rock gently as chunky oars slip from your hands. The jagged blue line becomes flat as your body settles down for the death rattle. And you're OK with that; in fact, you beckon.

But then there is a shaking. Shaking. Goddamn, someone is shaking you. It's the daughter. "Damn, Victoria. Damn, you are obnoxious."

TAPE 21
SIDE B

There is hardly any dessert more popular with the male members of the family than good, old-fashioned pie.
—The Occident Flour Company

"**W**ake *up, Mommy. Mommy, can you hear me? MOMMY! MOM!"*

And her eyes are cold slate. Unforgiving.

She looks at me and says, "I haven't graduated yet. I haven't had my first orgasm. I can't bake apple pie." She is stubborn. Shining in her anger—spinning her healing vortex in a whirl I can't escape. I just want to sleep. My neck is swollen and purple. Suddenly I'm scared. Not for me but for her.

I look up and say, "Men like pie."

I read that in a ladies' magazine.

I can't teach you how to make things from apples. I never took the time to learn.

The intensive care nurse holds a tube and my wrist, which has begun to pulse. She drops my arm.

Victoria doesn't cry; she gets rigid and crinkles up around the nose and eyes. She stares me down in a game of eyeball chicken. I cower beneath the sheet. I'll lose this game.

I think of my pineapple cookie jar. Two of the green leaves are broken off and I forgot to buy Crazy Glue. Inside the jar are two boxes of green tea and four foil-wrapped Valiums.

I tell Victoria to go home and have milk and cookies.

She says I better be there in the morning when she comes back.

She'll be pissed if I die without her permission.

I am fully awake now, and the morphine offers little solace to the ragged burn I feel as the cancer pips and pops beneath my skin. Bitch-bastard-son of a mother-fucker-crazy-skeet-shoot. Each gobble becomes a twitchy dig beneath my ribs. I imagine the marrow turning black or green as the cancer molders and melts me into tar.

I can't. I can't stand another minute. I flip channels on the hospital TV, hoping someone will tell me how to die nicely. Tell me how to die; help me die. That's what I was thinking. I even tried to practice panic numbness. Nothing. A scream sobs, catches in my windpipe like a rocket balloon, spinning and long. Oozing blue hot air.

EEEEeeeeichfffffft.

A teeny rip slips out. I taste the metal side rail, which I have been gnawing like a lollipop. How many licks to the center? My teeth ache beneath the gums. When I sleep, I dream of wisdom teeth crumbling like crackers—my mouth full of crumbs. Unable to whistle.

It is morning and Victoria is livid. She thinks I'm being lazy about life. Thinks I should try. She reminds me of the Harrisburg Marathon we ran last year. She wanted to quit. She was crying and dragging on my arm. I said no. This is Boston. Whatever that means. I told her to suck it up and keep running. She did. Two of her toenails fell off and the bottoms of her feet were bloody, but she ran for me.

A daughter's revenge.

I tell her this is more like a Triple Ironman, back to back to back with no food or water. With weights strapped on. Hundreds of pounds. Broken kneecaps.

"Whatever," she says and flips through a movie magazine. She's looking for the crossword puzzle. I pretend to sleep, but I can hear her scribble on the paper.

She tapes a poem onto the pink plastic water pitcher. It's about dreams and races. She writes about hating pie and loving my peanut soup. I throw up into the kidney shaped vomit catcher.

That night she reads me our favorite Dr. Seuss book. Yertle the Turtle. I know how Mack feels.

Victoria stands there inside her folded arms as if she is holding her ribs together. She's trying to look tough to scare me better, but I know that if she unfolds her arms she will begin to fall apart.

"Well?" She says this as if I know the answer. The right corner of her lips turns down slightly, just like mine. We are not symmetrical.

"Well?"

"You sound like a pep rally." I know this will piss her off. "Rah rah sis boom bah." I giggle. Victoria relaxes enough to know that I let her win. A-4 Battleship. Someone waves a white hanky.

So I checked myself out of St. Mary's on a Wednesday. It was October 31st and it was snowing half mixed with sleet so there was this eerie Christmas-creepy feel to the air. I had Vic drive me up and down the streets at a crawl. I hung out of the window like a dog so the flakes could sting my cheeks. I watched kids dressed as ninjas and witches. They ran around in a flurry of plastic hair, swords, and rubber warts.

Vic knew I loved October with the red snap leaves and the smiling pumpkin heads, but this time it was different. It seemed spiritual somehow. Like a prayer. She kept driving round the blocks because I asked. Not so much asked but waved. Waved her on. We drove until I couldn't feel my face and the pain was a pinpoint of sharp in my side. I think she thought maybe I was actually going to die during that bizarre drive. After about three hours, I cranked up the window and we pulled into Nickel's Brake and Muffler. They were closed but I needed to get out.

I felt the last bit of morphine leaking in droplets from my lids as the pain began to slash at me in waves. I remember thinking it was a bit like labor without the pushing and silly breath patterns. No nurses there trying to tell you a fluff of air will ease the pain.

I was a torn womb. I felt as though my insides were tearing bit by bit with each step.

Then it became deep. It felt as if I were walking on spikes.

I thought of the divorce, of that time before the cancer when I imagined that this knickknack or that was important somehow. Or that half was mine no matter what.

I had been an old drama queen.

Suddenly. Everything but Victoria and Nick felt like bullshit. So I got out of the car dressed in hospital slippers and bib overalls. I stuck my head through the driver's side window and gave my baby a butterfly kiss on her closed eyelids.

I half jogged half sobbed eighteen blocks home. I felt as if I had to prove something but wasn't sure what. Vic was driving behind me. She was huddled over the steering wheel, sort of hugging it to herself. She put on classic rock as loud as it would play. *So you run from the shelter of your mother's little helper. Dew-dew-dew-do-do-do-do-do-duh duh-duh-duh-duh-da-do.*

My life began to have a soundtrack. In that moment of time, things started to reel into sections of scenes and edited bits, which I could enter at any time inside my head. I started to write out scenarios. *Act 1, Scene 1: Woman heals self.*

We sat at the kitchen bar. I made a to-do list.

1. Check into holistic health clinic.
2. Cancel chemotherapy treatment.
3. Order juicer for carrot detox.
4. Buy a bowl of goldfish and a box turtle.
5. Set up daily massage appointments.
6. Laugh.
7. Chant.
8. Watch *I Love Lucy* reruns.
9. Soak in sea salt and milk.
10. Drink two gallons of purified water every day.
11. Walk in the ocean.

The doctor called.
Mom called.
I unplugged the phone.
It worked. Anyway, I didn't acknowledge the sickness.

My ideas were not unique; in fact, I'm sure that I read them somewhere, but like everything else I read, heard, or saw, it became difficult to tell what thoughts were originally mine.

Fortunately, alternative healing was big money back then. Still is. Salesmen sold me macrobiotic cookware. Organic steam tables.

I stopped throwing up.

"Mind over matter" became my mantra.

Or maybe it was the hookah. Who knows?

But I love a good cliché to live my life by.

By Christmas that year, I wasn't yellow with jaundice. Aunt Jen stopped bringing by gooey blueberry muffins.

Mom's church took me off the prayer list. My skin turned pink.

Victoria sold her first painting.

Nicholas bought a guitar.

I published a series of healing books, which were peppered with experiential anecdotes. Some pundits said I was a quack; others said I was a healer. All I knew was that the pain was like an amputated foot: gone but there in spirit.

TAPE 22
SIDE A

I never went back to my work in pharmaceuticals. I puttered around growing lavender and cats claw, which I sold from the back of my house and later from a boutique on Elm Street. On weekends, I traveled around to book signings and speaking engagements. It was profitable so I kept doing it.

I was making money but never felt home. I'd lie there on the hotel sheets thinking of all the one-night stands in all the world and I realized that I was going through a phase. A short-lived affair with extreme nothingness. It was a simplistic way to live. Sell. Drink. Sleep.

I drank salty dogs and red eyes in nondescript hotel bars from London to Idaho. Before long, the bars began to feel like home. Everyone was there for the same sorry-lonely-business-sex-type reasons. Elbows propped. Heels leaned. A giant human pretzel; we merged at predictable bends and knots.

It's the same no matter. Behind the half wall, weary bartenders fold napkins, scoop olives, mash fruit, and shake various numb mixtures. They are mundane because it's easier that way. They are flirty because the rent is due. They have honed their ability to look like they give a shit about what you are saying. All the while selling you up to a more expensive drunk. I guess in a way they're kind of like window dancers and we are a sad sack audience constantly pressing our faces to the glass.

Look, look, she actually reads poetry like me.

Look, look, he thinks I have good taste.

I loved to watch those veteran bartenders.

Danny from the Irish bar in Hollywood—skinny, mirthless and dry. Drank whiskey on his Cheerios. Charged tourists double. Let the locals in for free. Pulled out a thirty-aught-six when Colin from Scotland got smashed and got pissed because one of the barbacks kept asking him the same question. "What day is it, Colin?" Half-second pause. "It's Sean Connery's Birt-day." I gave him yarrow root and detox tea for his mom. Drinks on the house.

Ken from New Zealand, displaced in Miami. Mean. Bloody knuckle mean. Best burger on South Beach. He refused to make piña coladas, rumrunners or mudslides (otherwise known as pussy drinks). I slept with him every couple of months. Good PR.

These guys had this sort of "fuck you, I control your poison" attitude. I loved that, which is why I hung around listening.

Most of them needed their jobs to pay for babies, books, or biology classes. There was a feeling of leaving as if their foot was half out the door yet they never seemed to make it.

They got hit on and whistled at but rarely stiffed. It was fascinating to see the sleight of hand twitching away extra fives from cheapskates.

Social graces are merely an act.

I told you so.

I told you so.

Every night from happy hour to 2 a.m., we enter darkened rooms. We hide our eyes so hands may slide up thighs. Doctors, lawyers, teachers, PTAers, husbands, wives, ministers, and pastry chefs get back to the basics.

we want to be
need to be fucked
to be
needed to be
lied to

Camaraderie in a glass.

I began to feel as if I were sitting with rows of clothed skeletons. Teeth clacking up and down, up and down. Tongues snaking in and out, in and out. Ankles crossed. Ass bones scraped. Jaw. Jaw. Jaw.

Fluid in the throat. Walk to bathroom. Reflex to gag.

I became friends with Danny and Ken. I'd sit there in their darkest corner ordering shot after shot of tequila with two drops of Tabasco. I scratched holes in napkins, which I plugged with twenty-dollar tips. Sometimes fifty if the jokes were good.

We became a funky group of drifting loners. The ones you hear about after murders.

He kept to himself.

She didn't have any friends.

We didn't really like people and sort of tolerated each other by telling stories about living on rafts or up in trees. We sent money to people who sat in trees to prove points.

I'm like that now. The boys send me shot glasses from wherever they go on their two-week vacations. The collection rotates on an old watch display turntable by the window. One has a shark that lights up when you plunk it down.

I am their charity tree hugger here in my condo island. Save the two hundred-year-old tree woman. Bucket up tuna and marshmallows. The chainsaw buzzes just below. Eventually, we'll all fall down.

Dan sends copies of Hemingway and Kerouac. We talk of blowing up penises and shooting elephants just for the tusks. He's writing a novel about this Irish family in the 1800s—back when it wasn't cool to be Irish.

I email him. Kerouac is crap, I say. He lived off his mama. Took money from his girlfriend. World adventurer? Believe what you like, little brother. I can read moocher lit.

The phone rings.

I don't answer.

Bitch, get down from there.

Who the fuck

Do you think

You are

Making my life

Inconsequential

But I don't. I'm still here in the multi-colored cushions. Covering my body parts. Waiting to slaughter lambs or first-born sons or talk to burning bushes.

Danny reminds me via email that this is a luxury. I know. I am lucky to have money in some imaginary space in some bank on Washington Street in some city. I perch on the buoyancy of zeros.

What if a virus wipes me out?

I guess I'll get a real life, a real job like I used to have. As per Congress, according to law, paid for by me.

This is what they wait for.

The moment of Bankruptcy that will make me hand over the keys to a new CEO.

TAPE 23
SIDE B

Say say now playmate, come out and play with me and we'll be bonney three, slide down my apple tree. Climb up my porch step into my cellar door and we'll be jolly friends for ever more, more, more!
—playground song, as chanted in 1970
on the Halifax Elementary School Playground

I can live on bean sprouts. They grow in the window with cherry tomatoes and chocolate peppermint.

I tell this to Mom when she starts pestering me about Thanksgiving. "It's family time," she says into my earphone, in postcards, via email. *Come to dinner.* Thursday at six. Roast turkey and real cranberry sauce. Dad will pick you up.

And he will try, I'll give him that. Every year, he tries. He drives over in the tan Impala he's had for thirty years. Sits below and honks as if I'm his date. I go to the window and wave him home.

It will take more than cranberry sauce.

Shit.

Every year, the kids bring me fake turkey from the gourmet vegetarian food mart off Jackson Square. I drink; they check in. I scratch Nicholas's back and write him checks for college, car insurance, and fast food. I bake oatmeal cookies and make him cream of wheat for breakfast.

Victoria shows me scanned renderings of her latest paintings. On Black Friday, we Christmas shop online or from catalogues. I furnish their apartments and buy them new cars.

This year they mention lingerie and easels. They decline my push for all things straightforward. I don't want them to be like me.

I speak of jump ropes and scooters. Six pounds of chocolate will be here for the stockings. I miss having little kids.

Every time they come, I am surprised. They say it is good to be quiet for a few days. Peace on earth once a year. But I see Nicholas jittery on the phone. He goes to pubs when we sleep. Comes back smelling of Swisher Sweets and Absolut with grapefruit.

Victoria hangs new artwork above my shoe wall. She accidentally knocks down a row of stilettos and winds up trying them on for half a day. I go online to order her sixteen pairs in different colors and styles. I love her, but she can't have my shoes. She's gotta have her own vibe. I know just what to get her.

I know my babies will soon marry or find lovers who'll be freaked out by me. They'll stop coming to eat turkey and watch football. Or maybe come for just lunch then leave. They'll call from payphones. I know this. I tell them it's OK.

"Go with Dad," I say, hoping they will not.

"It's fine," I say, knowing it's not.

"Is he still with her?"

"Yes, Mom."

I hate her for her youth.

They try to appease my wrinkled brow. I love them for their white lies and fake turkey.

Mom says they patronize me. She says if they'd stop coming to visit then I'd come out. As if opening the door to smog and crime will make me OK.

I tell her she's a crazy.

A fusty branch.

Someday you'll understand. She weeps onto my answering machine.

My eyes ache with frustration. Give me a second to clear my head. I just want things to line up. To stand in order.

I don't understand anything and nothing makes sense. I don't see the way. The truth. The life.

I tell her this via email greeting. This is how we communicate. She leaves a message. I change the greeting with quotes from Plato. And I'm stuck on him lately. And I don't know why.

A *M*A*S*H* marathon. Again.

She calls back but I let the answering machine pick up. And up and up.

Beep.

TAPE 24
SIDE A

Milk is the best mustache. It does more things for us than any other food we eat. Milk helps to make strong bones. Milk helps to make good teeth. Milk helps to make strong muscles. Milk tastes good. Drink plenty of milk. It is a fine thing for growing children to have a glassful of milk at breakfast, a glassful of milk at lunch, and a glassful of milk at suppertime. A glass of warm milk just before you go to bed will help you to sleep better.

—*Growing Big and Strong*
1939

Leave a message and I'll email you back as soon as possible. If this is the furniture guys, please be sure to deliver my sectional add-ons before the holidays. I need a rollaway bed as well.

Beep.

Shugahr, shugahr... pick up the phone.

I don't.

She bangs down her end. She thinks she can make me behave. Put me in pleated plaid skirts and sit me down. Make me be good.

I swear she thinks I'm nine. I don't know why we talk.

Leave.

Me.

Alone.

I send her hush money. She won't stop calling. She sends back the check or says she gave it to God. A tithe. I feel like she's hanging on my ankles—so heavy I can do nothing but shuffle.

Cankles.

Chain gang mama.

Yesterday I read a health zine. It says that cow's milk makes the stomach lining bleed in babies and toddlers. It can cause digestive problems and has lots of steroids and antibiotics. We aim to be a nation of giants. The NFL has never been so big, so full of testosterone. I wonder if Terrell would be such an ass with broken hipbones or rips in his liver. I wonder if milk could fix that.

They are supposed to bring the new additions to my couch tomorrow. Really, Dr. Jones, you should see this room: two thousand square feet of nothing but sectional cushions. You can't see any floor. There are ladders and even a porch swing hanging or attached to portions. I may break the world record for staying on a single couch for the longest time.

The fattest guy in the world holds the record for staying inside. When he dies, they'll bring a crane to wrench his carcass into the blue air.

Yesterday the Guinness Book guy came with his camera and recorder. I asked if he could put me beside the Indian man with the long fingernails. You should see this one. His fingernails are so long that he has to have two wives to wash, clean, and feed him. I wonder which woman wipes his ass. Her picture isn't in the book. Just him. Smiling with polka dot nails hanging from his fingers like curled Christmas ribbon. It used to be just the one hand but then this upstart from Saxton started growing his nails. Not much of a loser, Claude grew out his other hand and both feet. No one had ever done that before. So now he can't do anything but watch TV. He can't even feed himself. But he is in the book of records. There's always that. And his wives. What do they have to show for all the wiping?

Mom had a preacher friend like that. He used to put witty sayings on the outside church sign: "Hell is hotter-n-August tar—Come into the cool!" He loved sweet corn and Mom's homemade sourdough bread. Every Sunday, he got fatter. He always took seconds and thirds.

So anyhow, Dr. Jones, I bid on the next-door condo. I might as well expand. I was thinking of putting a garden and a water fountain with koi and naked pissing fairies in the middle of this circle.

At night when I crawl along the cushions, I get a craving for nature. I'll buy plastic deer and pink flamingos. Maybe some stuffed squirrels and latex macaws or rubber fish that flip and talk on walls. Better yet, maybe a stuffed grizzly.

Batteries for toys.

Curved things.

I'll furrow a trail through a knocked-out hole in the wall that separates me from the guy next door. Turns out dot coms weren't so profitable. He's selling everything.

I should've told him you can't sell nothingness forever. It has to be a thing that arrives in packages with throwaway wrappings. Well, first you have to create a service or a craving need. Lucky for me, I got Congress to pass that "Love Your Laptop" Day. It's the first Tuesday of September.

Right. What kind of holiday is that?

Who wants to celebrate cubicles and word processors?

Real people want personalized programs with little pop-up sidekicks. Sort of like paper dolls with clip-art body parts. They need beautiful creations that talk and flirt in the corner of a screen. The first demo was named Belle. I got two thousand orders for her all-blonde program. The second demo was her twin sister, brunette Jennifer with bigger titties.

Oddly, the bulk of my orders are for the boy dolls.

Ted, who is a normal-sized blonde and intelligent looking. He doesn't say much. He's the cheaper version. Mostly poets and artists order him.

And then there is Theo. He's tall with brown hair and vivid blue or brown eyes. He says what you want to hear.

You look skinny today.

You are beautiful.

Will you have my baby?

Marry me.

I'm a millionaire.

Most of my clients order the full June Ward package, which can be accessed via high-speed connection only. You point. Click. Say hello to your alternate ego or techno spouse slash lover. No more lonely chunks of eight-hour days. There's always someone to talk to in the land of fake people.

If you buy the whole package, you can get a spouse who brings you nice bits of news on the hour or weight loss tips or how to grow your money market. He or she will say nothing about plane crashes or wars. And certainly no international shit. But he or she will relate tutorials on eyebrow tweezing and Christmas wreaths.

Clients send profiles. If they are career parents, then I send info on the advantages of quality time over quantity time. If they're single parents, I have the toy espouse the values of one-on-one time over two-parent time. If it's a stay-at-home parent, I plug in bits about de-socialization and home schooling.

I get $39.95 a month and someone somewhere feels useful and loved. As if their choices are valid and correct, and if not are perhaps close to choices c, d, or all of the above. People need to be right about their lives because that's all there is.

Rightness requires wrongness.

Anyway, it's going well, the startup parent company Rubberspouse.com fills so many with a sense of meaning. It's like having a dog but better.

I'm also having a sale on laptop accessories that come with birth certificates of authenticity for little kids. It's kind of like the Cabbage Patch phenomenon and seems to go over well with those born in the eighties. Each laptop I sell gets its own name and sex. I think it's weird how everything must be gendered. But it must. The boy laptops are blue and the girls pink. Not really innovative on my part. Nothing new under the sun! Thank you, King Solomon.

TAPE 25
SIDE A

Hair trend alert. Everyone's Going Dark!

—*Life and Style*
December 2006

S o I'm buying more real house space for computers and couches. I bid $200,000 on the apartment next door, which is a great deal. The guy who lived there on weekends has bottomed out. His credit is maxed out. Every day, collectors from around the world call or send letters requesting that he pay up now or they'll sue him. I expect him to blow his brains out very soon. I should lend him my Uzi. I put in a much better offer before all of this happened. He waited too long. Made the call after things were wrong. I feel bad. I do. But a penny saved ...

I have worked out the plans on an interactive web site. The architect is from Alaska. We'll knock out all the walls. The ceilings will be supported by dismantled oil derricks. I'll paint a mural on the rooftop.

It will be a story that begins in the center of a grape-lipped Mother Earth. She's being raped by sun-yellow mini-vans and Hummers. Children wave octane candy canes as they bump above the pregnant wheels, which have ballooned like a Speed Buggy cartoon.

Do you remember that car? It had eyes and every time the bad guys'd push it from a cliff, the wheels would pop out and float Speed Buggy down the river.

Her hips yawn. Baby baskets. They clench bloody gee-gaws and Mardi Gras beads. She doesn't cry or spit death rain upon her mawkish children. She is bereaved and sighing like a motor-oiled swan.

The mural is sectioned like Japanese anime. Right to left. In squares. Segment two, she crawls and claws at her clotted fingers. She bites tire tread baubles like Tootsie Rolls.

Sucks out the center.

Next, she crouches like a track star—legs crooked back, head front and center. Shoulders rolled. Next, she runs. One fist clenches fiery hair. She rips it from her head in clumps that bead on her lip.

She implodes. Takes everything, inverted like a vacuuming volcano. Flying shrimp and cows swirl in the suck of her lungs as she reels. Babies, coconut trees, macaroons, stovepipe hats, high-tops, evergreens, libraries, monarchs, red worms, stockings, mud, puddles, boxes, turtles. Living things bubble and crawl beneath her skin. She becomes translucent like a baby pigeon. Intestines and heart red and beating. Sometimes purple. Blobs of corn slide down to that indigestible place.

She retches up batch after batch of cookie dough, politicos, pundits, and presidents. They are speckled with chocolate chips and eggshells. Parts of budgets. Coupons.

Tadpoles squirm in dinosaur footprints.

In the final square, there is a black hole. It is as I imagine it to be. Full of invisible things and nothing things. All you see is a crab of knuckles here or there, sort of fading. It is gray into black. A something unrecognizable because it is a nose on our face.

I'm convinced there should be no form. Just a nothing that you can't stay out of or step over. Something like black crayon over houses and families of four. The ones you interpret in kindergarten.

See, Dr. Jones? I can't get out of my head. That's the problem, isn't it? Or is it?

I was shopping for pesto and hash browns on a Sunday. It was one of those chains. Huge with orange and brown lettering. Plump old ladies in net caps stood at the ends of rows, cooking little sausages wrapped in dough or handing out cubes of speckled cheese. The music was oozing and pleasant, but you couldn't detect the tune. I was pushing a metal cart and the front wheel kept squabbling madly like a hound dog head. Sniffing the buffed floor for dirt.

I got to the sugar row.

Brown.
Powdered.
Granulated.
Red and green for cookies.
Liquid.
Fake.
Organic.
Rough brown.
Packets.
Boxes.
Ten-pound bags.
Store brand.
I looked at my list. There was sugar. But what kind? I couldn't remember why we needed these things or how many so I put one of each kind of sugar into the cart, which didn't leave room for much else.

There was a bag of Idaho potatoes in my basket. Who decided to spell it with or without an e? Who named it potato? Who invented so many words for the same thing?

I remember thinking that I missed the grunts and burps. It was probably someone who wanted a brown leg of bear instead of black and an uumph wouldn't do. So bear became a circle on the wall. A scratching on paper. Triangles began to mean something. Things began to be exact. Had to be formed. "A"s to look like "a"s.

Kings paid scribes. We believed what they said. Or didn't and then built pencil factories. Rows and rows of toddlers sitting on multicolored chairs writing ovals of "O"s and "A"s. Getting it right. Finally getting it. And then sitting desolate on a pile of sand. Forgetting castles and goose flapping and how fun it is to scribble nothing but sworls.

Then growing up.
Sitting in plastic chairs.
Graduating.
Sitting in plastic chairs.
Retiring.
Sitting in plastic chairs.

The manager wore an orange vest with a brown tie to match the cashiers. He shook my shoulder lightly. "Closing time." An awkward-polite smile. The carts were fitted into each other in a long row of metal. I'd been there for seven hours. Staring at the sugar.

"Maybe you should be in the nut row." He said this with a hopeful humor, as if trying to break the ice. He was awkward, hoping I wouldn't pull out a gun. My hands were resting in my jacket pockets.

"A person ought to be able to stop anywhere anytime and think for as long as they need."

I saw his name was Andrew. Tagged to his lapel. Andrew.

He had that scared "she's crazy" look and sort of motioned to the security guy by yawning and then crooking his finger behind his head. S.O.S.

I started pushing my cart. The wheel screeched and clattered. He walked sort of diagonal from me, closer to the rows of ribs and thighs.

"I suppose they have knives back there?" I stopped near the Oreo cookies and u-turned back towards the seafood deli. I had this sudden craving for squid.

And that's when things got weird. Andrew started running and shouting, "Lady, hey lady! This is serious. Now. Everybody out by 10. Store policy. See those cameras? My job. Out. Get out!"

And right by the Double Stuf Oreos I rammed my cart into the corner display food pyramid. Plastic packages crunched under my Birkenstocks. Andrew fell to his knees and began stacking cookie packs back where they belonged, as if the world was falling apart. Call 911! Call 911!

I ran out. Straight to the ATM, which always reminds me of Pong. Bloop. $100. Bloop-bloop. Negative balance. My palms ached from clenching the metal cart. I punched in my 1-9-7-7 PIN code for money. I was still thinking about seafood and where I might get some at that hour.

And then I had this falling feeling. The money spilt out of a slot and I felt dizzy. What if it didn't come out or never did? What if the balance was nothing but zeros or I forgot my code? Social. Security. Yeah. Right. What if the numbers disappear?

Then what?

I called off work for a week. Balancing checkbooks. Erasing numbers. Tearing out statement pages. Everything seemed wobbly. Off-kilter. Dizzy-like.

So I sat. On the chintz couch, which was too ugly to be unreal. It functioned as my seeing eye dog, the thing that was stable where I wasn't.

At first I welcomed my hole space as I began to climb inward. There was a hardness, a sort of solidity. A lump of coal or diamond. Something to feel or know.

I became unreal to everyone else.

A disembodied voice on the phone.

Zeros and ones on a balance sheet.

Computer password.

Account number.

IM Icon.

A figment.

I wish I really were that floaty ever-changing thing. A soap bubble. Something to be popped. A rainbow slick that cannot feel the cancer in its squamous row along my spine. Hateful. Real. Squid tentacles suctioning up my spine. Pancreas hard as knots.

TAPE 25
SIDE B

Real or Faux? Bumps are popping out all over Hollywood. But who's really pregnant?

—*Life and Style*
December 2006

I give up on power yoga and wheat-grass juice. I dump the antioxidants down the toilet as if they are cocaine crystals that made my nose bleed. The free radicals swirl beneath my skin like vicious goblins. Vitamin C can't touch this ugly.

I chain-smoke and type instant messages at my recliner chair slash desk. I think of eating raw filet mignon. Perhaps I'll give the cancer a boost. I think of Brazilian trees falling somewhere far away as I chew the meat. I apologize to the macaw. Parrots hate me far and away. I order a caseload of gourmet meat.

Maybe I could plant some trees here to make up for my transgression. Perhaps cut a hole in the roof for giant pines and oaks. I could bring in dump trucks of topsoil. Plant the seedlings. It's not so crazy. Malls grow palm trees right in the food court. The high-rises in Aventura look like Babylon with their waving rooftop palms.

I had my lawyer make some phone calls. He's ordered my forest and contacted the gardeners. But then that damn Susie Sanchez from Channel 7 got wind of my plans. She has created a firestorm media invasion. Knocking, calling, emailing, and writing. White vans with silver satellite dishes paced along the sidewalk. Camera lenses began to snout along the borders—looking for truffles.

Somehow or another they've found out that I'm the sole owner of Rubberspouse but more importantly that I'm rich and haven't been out of my apartment for years.

The guy from "Moneytalk" wanted an interview. I told him I'd send a spokesperson. He wasn't happy about that, but I said he could put my high-school yearbook picture on the background. First thing they ask is if I'm actually building an indoor forest. I was on the phone with them and laughed.

My laugh is the only thing I love about myself. It tinkles and roars all together. People get mesmerized. We wind up butt fucking ourselves crazy. So I agreed to come out of seclusion the following Friday. Of course I didn't. I mean, yeah, I said I would, but I didn't.

Instead, I sent Derek. He went in drag, as me with extension string bean hippie hair. Sandals with socks. A silk pink skirt with iron-on peace sign patches. He was like a beautiful, young Dame Edna. He talked about the weirdness of living alone, gave some stock advice (Buy Hershey, Disney, Google; Sell ABC, CBS, and FOX). He flipped his hair a great deal and flirted with the cameramen. Ratings skyrocketed. The fake me became a regular on the show. The invasion of my invisible privacy is intolerable.

Mom thinks I shouldn't have used a queer to stand in for me.

TAPE 26
SIDE A

Aries (March 2 to April 19): You hunger for excitement as unruly Uranus hot-wires Mars. Mellow out with a cool-blue pressed shadow. Guerlain Divinora Radiant Colour Palette 4 Shade in Touche de Brume, $55, NeimanMarcus.
—Stylescopes by Astologer Karen Christino
for the week of December 18-December 24th

So far, today has been fan-fuggin-tastic! I got the condo for my sectional extension. The couch is beginning to remind me of a giant plastic Cootie toy with screw-on purple and green midsections and yellow antennae skewered up and out. It now winds around the living room into where the bedrooms used to be. Every section touches the next. There isn't anywhere left to turn.

Yesterday, Mom asked me when it would end. So I told her that it's kind of like those paper chain gingerbread men we used to cut. Hand to index to thumb. Folding people spill out into an origami accordion. My couch is like that. I just pull on a corner and out pops a new wrinkle. It's something I hadn't really noticed before. I told her it was my own personal performance piece. She said, "Do you mean like the Nutcracker?"

Fuggin.

Fuggin is my new favorite word. I got it from a chat group called VampsRus.org. It's a teen goth site. I log on pretty much every day to talk about fairies, piercings, spikes, and hair glue. I told everyone I had a fauxhawk and a clit ring, so they let me into their chat clique. The oldest kid in the group calls herself Eekin. She says she's fifteen. I call myself Knot and tell them I'm seventeen. We talk about prosthetics and the value of fake teeth. I point out that black lipstick is passé. We talk about hair extensions and fat suction. Inanimate objects. The blackness around the eyes—the punched holes in ears and noses. Belt buckles and needle fangs. Most of them say they're not religious. They believe in Satan. Which is of course the same as believing in God.

It's funny that I love this room. I love the blanket acceptance. I love the fake age—the name—the youth. I love the fact that I am seventeen and full of angst and crappy poetry. I love the fact that I can pretend to have some kind of integrity here. In this imaginary space.

This kid Eekin started emailing me outside the chat room. She says she connects to me more than the others. I talk to her because she is suicidal.

Her mom's thinking of putting her in a mental hospital.

Eekin used a pocketknife to outline crypts and sunflowers on the tops of her feet. She carved her skin and then shaded it with hot match tips for a puckered effect. She did this during the winter so that by Easter Sunday her scabs had congealed and scarred into a permanent sculpture. She said it was like 3-D without the glasses. It reminded her of an ancient graveyard.

At first, I didn't believe her, because who knows what you really get in these chat rooms? But then she scanned me a picture of her ink-word feet. The skin was mushroom brown. I stared at the crypts and gargoyles she had carved.

She told me.

Strapped in sandals to Easter mass. Her mom didn't notice until they knelt for wafers. Now everyone thinks she's crazy because she slopped up Father Kelly's offering of Christflesh and blood.

She wore eggshell blue. It was a dress from the JC Penney's sale at the mall.

A ladybug hopscotched down the rafters to the mirror of Eekin's eyes. Livid red-white and gray tombs echoed in the balcony. Eekin took out her knife and started carving the path the ladybug took.

Someone screamed.

Instant replay...

Eekin unwinds a piece of Bazooka Original pink bubblegum.

Chews.

Adds the beetle.

Chews.

Blows a monstrous bubble flecked with bits of leg and chips of orange.

Chews.

Polka dot gum.

Chews.

Pocks a pipping snap of sugar.

Chews.

Plucks the glob and sticks it between the onionskin pages of the red hymnal.

Her teeth grind out Jesus songs.

Immobilized.

They speed down I-83 in the blue Toyota-Hyundai-Chevy. It is a boxy car with four doors, pastel like the fake contacts her mother wears. They are driving too fast. The tires melt rubber tracks to the stoplight at the end of Warm Springs Avenue. Two cars and a delivery van full of keg beer and pretzel dough chug slowly to the red light.

Then the blue car full of crying Mother and Eekin skin screeching to a stop.

Eekin's ears ache like they did when she was little and full of infection. She unplugs her seatbelt. Thumbs open the door and tumbles onto the blacktop.

Run.

The sky is royal blue.

She beats her Mom back to their tan duplex. Metal butterflies are tacked in pink and green above the mailbox. The kitchen is egg yolk and Amish hues. Wooden cow magnets march with duck and chicken memorabilia on the walls. The napkin rings match the tea towels, which also match the curtains. A ham bastes in carrot juice. There will be applesauce today.

Eekin sits by the cat litter and sniffs, but even that is chemically enhanced to smell like roses. It is neatly clumped. Sifted and raked into sparkly globs of cat shit.

Chew.

A hole through her lip and the skin tastes like soup can lids.

Chew.

Blows crimson rust bubbles. She siphons the brick-red lip skin onto the frothy towels.

No longer perfect.

Chew.

The terrycloth fringe goes to pink. Soap blood hardens as it dries.

They lift her into the back seat.

The end. Just like that the end.

LOL. LOL.

She's always saying that. What does it mean?

What do you mean?

LOLOLOLOL at Mommy through the glass. The romper room swirly glass. Oh, this is sick. Am I sick? Do you think so? Am I? Sick?

Is what she typed.

Is what she said.

Is what I didn't know.

Should I help her, Dr. Jones?

Maybe I should invite her over for a few days. It would kill me, but I could do it. Of course. I could make chicken potpie soup. Pinch the egg and flour while we talk. Boil the marrow into the broth.

Drink bones. Drink bones.

Soak her razor toes in vanilla milk at my table.

Chai bones. Chai bones.

I betcha I know that mother of hers. She can't even help herself, much less that dying girl.

She's probably the clean-freak type who buys white plastic Christmas trees because she hates clumps of needles and brown things. They dangle blue or clear light bulbs. The limbs are leached of color. Everything is bright.

Forward.

Reply.

Reply all.

Say something.

Are you there?

My inbox is always empty.

I fold the three-ply toilet tissue into triangles to pass the time of day.

TAPE 27
SIDE A

Tara repaired bad surgery. What she changed. In 2004, botched plastic surgery left Tara Reid, now 31, with scar tissue around her breast implants and bulgy and uneven skin on her liposuctioned tummy. In September she went back under the knife to undo the damage and regain her self-esteem.

—*Life and Style*
December 2006

I'm having a camera installed so I can edit my days for you. It will be like the reality shows, only boring. Maybe I'll wear a bikini for you. I'm sure it'll beat talking stories into this ancient recorder. I'd like to be freer. I'll compress every hour into a couple of seconds so it's not so boring.

Yesterday, for example.

It was too long to speak about.

I woke up and leafed through magazines and catalogues as usual, admiring the lace-up corsets and push-up bras. After that, I ate a bran muffin with coffee and two tablespoons of peanut butter. Then I watched the morning shows.

Ran the treadmill from 10-11 a.m.

Stomach crunches, 12-1 p.m.

Ate some carrots.

Weight training, 1-2 p.m. (back and biceps).

Stationary bike, 2-3 p.m.

Weight training, 3-4 p.m. (legs and shoulders).

Rowing machine, 4-5 p.m.

Ate some water and drank my celery juice.

Weight training, 5-6 p.m. (chest and triceps).

Fat-free Healthy Choice, 6-7 p.m. (mustard soup).

Stretches, 7-8 p.m. (power yoga).

Sleep, 8 p.m. to morning.

Today I can't move. Not a bit.

I'm lying on the peach section with my laptop on my belly like an inverted fetus.
DSL.
Check on Eekin.
Key-tap-kaa-tap.
Tap-click-ka-tap.
I've got mail.
No shit!
Reply.
Forward.
Mom—delete.
Bank—send.

Eekin: hey
Knot: LO
Eekin: laughing out? What?
Knot: o I thought that was short for hello
Eekin: how old r u really?
Knot: :)) double chin
Eekin: seriously be serious u rnt 17 ru?
Knot: more like 50 something sorry
Eekin: jeeze what r u a freak? Why r u here
Knot: im a hermit a recluse I don't leave the house so don't worry u r Safe.
Eekin: :(…
Knot: its been 3 yrs I've been here
Eekin: r u kra Z
Knot: I think so I don't know I pay a shrink
Eekin: can I meet U
Knot: I'm shriveled you would be scared. I'm like an apple doll all wrinkled and sour soft.
Eekin: can I have your address? Hurry mom's banging her Fendi-bender on my Door.
Knot: you know it
Eekin: don't know shit
Knot: 17 bourbon street
Eekin: in Manhattan? You kidding?
Knot: oh that's the address on my hall door. It's a twenty story condo. Old school short. Building. You know the Mackie building? Glass

and stone. Call from the box to 867-5309. Bring
cheerios, headphones, and a ball peen hammer.
Eekin: k bye.

TAPE 27
SIDE B

Baby News! Matt Lauer, 48, and wife Annette, 41, welcomed their third child together, baby Thijs (pronounced Tice), on November 28...

—*Life and Style*
December 2006

She's coming. Now. What did I do that? Hotdogs. Where are the hotdogs? Turkey dogs, veggie dogs. I'll just cook hotdogs. Tofu dogs. No. She might hate that. Maybe coffee and scones. Delivered scones from Redcoat's T-Shop. Toffees. Let's pretend we're English like Madonna.

Rewind.

"Hello." She hedges into the room.

I bluff-lean over the edge of the back of my monstrosity, which once felt creative—now feels like a hump-back. Something that cannot be leached or scalped away—certainly not explained. A camel.

She takes my hand, as if to pull me under. She climbs into my room and stands there, skinny and blue.

Her shoulders scoop inward, as if to hide her breasts. As if she can suck them into her androgynous spine. The loop of an army backpack is about to slide to her elbow, which will surely set her off-balance. She flips it back, unsure if she will stay or go. She smells of trees and cinnamon. Her mother bakes a lot. I know this from our online conversations. Cinnamon buns, sticky buns, pumpkin pie, and eggnog. She asks to take a shower. Kind of dares me, as there is no water in sight. I point to the place between two couch ends, just beneath the circular bed. She sees the door and disappears.

I am your fairy...

It takes her nearly two hours to scrape off the smell of cookies. Meanwhile, I refrigerate the food I have ordered. I put out a pot of hazelnut and I write a poem for Eekin on the back of an unbleached coffee filter:

Sheet rock
I woke up blank
Tried to write about peace and dirt
Or the lack of evergreens
Played Springsteen on the CD
Ate oatmeal
4 grams of fiber
ladled my whiteness into pudding
a saltless stew of water
stir and taste
spit
ran six miles
in silver rubber tread
my life is a soap
turning living and restless
on the hour every hour
my back is lined with borders
and festering chocolate sores

"You have an endless supply of hot water. I couldn't use it up." She sways. No longer blue—now pink—wearing black with plastered-down raven hair and smelling faintly of vinegar.

She stands there and reads my poem as she grabs my mellow whiskey. She gurgles it as if it were mouthwash. Haaarssh. Chhhheeep. She acts as if she can make silk milk or bee pollen from the rotgut.

"What does this mean?" My poem flutters.

"It means I've been watching too much of the news lately. It means death, war, religion, suicide, or suburbia. Or Black Friday. It means that I'll probably spend the next day or three in a tie-dye shirt listening to sixties music. It means that I don't know what to say to you. I don't know what is appropriate. I used to know that—the right thing to say. But I don't. So yeah, I mean no."

"So?" She tips back the bottle.

So typically teenager, I almost laugh.

So typically suicidal, I almost cry.

"So? So... The only thing I know for sure is that I will brew coffee in the morning and you will be here or not, but I will drink the brew. That's all I know. I may cook eggs or oatmeal, but that isn't a sure thing. I mean, I wish I were like Oprah with her sureness. I mean, I think you have to be a god to reach that state of knowing. And I'm more of an agitation to that way of thinking. It's the curse of several generations. Knowing what you are as defined by the label at the base of your skull. But beyond that, knowing nothing and being immobilized by the lack of one specific thing that might hold things together.

It is why I stay inside. Otherwise, the drift will never end. It is why we do Paxil, Celexa, and Prozac.

Her shoulders slump back as she finds the farthest spot from me. The backpack is between her ankles. I think she needs a nap—a good sleep. She looks at me as if I should lead or answer or say kill or not kill. Abort or not. Breathe or not.

"Say eggs or oatmeal."

A big mistake, I think to myself. A girl who wants to know things from the one who never knew or will ever know.

"Stay away from CNN, tarot cards, SATs, nylons, and missionaries."

"Plans are for the birds," she reads. This is tacked to one of my easels. I've been painting this powerful jetliner. Torrid blue. New York to Paris. A sparrow flies into the engine. A monkey wrench. Below, in a kitchen of taupe, a woman stirs her first cup of coffee.

"You really like your coffee, huh?" she says. "Starbucks is OK," she says.

It was the point of things. For so long.

The exact location of not getting it. "Um, yeah... Would you like to lie down?"

She nods. I sort of walk around on the cushions, which is the only way to get there. I try not to freak her out or make her run. She follows me through an overhang of indoor ivy into the place where the ladder goes up to the bed. It's the only one I have; I rarely use it. The sheets are stiff and clean but old. A box fan burrs in the corner to block the street sounds. I plug in the CD player and hand her headphones— assuming I know everything there is to know about teenagers. Knowing nothing. She shreds herself naked—back to me. Grabs a teddy bear and a giant white T-shirt. Both are worn through with light. Unplugs the player, turns off the fan. Lies rigid in the stream of sirens and footsteps. A car screeches. A man says, "Fuck off!" Eekin gently slumbers.

TAPE 28
SIDE A

Below, I feel dumber than dumb. Dumber than the movie or even the guy who thought up the movie or the ones who watched the movie. Damn stupid. I feel this deeply, as if it were a new form of arthritis, a sort of grind in an undiscovered brain joint.

I wander around the couch in circles, as if it is a string of prayer beads or Ikea Tibetan monk cushions. Ohm-one-ohm-two.

Crawl. Trawl. Tipeetoe.

A vortex rises like a vicious think tank that tears me up. I sort photographs from one shoebox to the other. I see her framed in white.

There is a Polaroid picture of a woman in striped polyester at a birthday party. Rocking. Cutting cake. Sliding candles into the buttermilk icing. One, one, the one is dying. She is grandmother. Mine. Her cervix is bruised from birthing so many. She leans a face onto her finger. A cheekbone plumps beneath her glasses, sweet and smelling of rising dough. Her lap rocks the world. Her womb is falling, torn and falling from the many, the all, the basket of herself. She hunches her shoulders to hide the breasts that fed the sway of all. She holds me on her knees. I crawl to her breast, to her mouth, to her grape-sweet neck. Wisdom tree. Her belly aches and cramps as it will on the table, later, when her cervix curls with cancer. She pulls me up and in. Strokes my tiny earlobes in amazement. "So perfect," she says. "So you."

I rummage through her pocketbook, which is large and black like a doctor bag. It is full of spearmint gum, peppermints and one unused red lipstick. Thirty-eight dollars in quarters, dimes and nickels, she lugged in that thing. You could stir it like metal soup or kill someone with the weight of it. "In case of emergency," she said. She carried that thing despite the pain. Folded me into herself.

How does one do that? Carry things for others?

I think this as Eekin sleeps above my head.

Is this my chance for the one thing I always wish for but never receive—the missing gene that makes a mother-woman give up her own lungs? To mother and get it right. To make up for things. To have something come naturally despite myself. To revel in the conch shell curve of an ear. Is this my time?

I don't know where that picture came from. Where did it hide? My Memmie.

Eekin slings from the ceiling in the ladder bed. She sleeps for days and days. She does not come down. I hold a mirror beneath her nose; it fogs. She lives.

TAPE 29
SIDE A

After two days, I sleep and dream of horrid things, metal wombs with no doors. All around are kidney-shaped bathtubs or vats. It's hard to tell which. They were huge and flat to the floor with swirling water; reminds me of hospital hot tubs.

I'm there. I'm waiting. In line by this rubber conveyor belt with old-fashioned glass bottles scattered around and lined on shelves. Each one is tagged like a toe. White stringed cards state $14.59 or $99.99. I'm waiting with a deli number. 83. The room with the whirring water is through double French glass doors. They steam and clear with the heat of the tubs.

A businessman waits beside me. He is impeccably gorgeous. Groomed smooth and carrying a buttery leather briefcase. He looks like the kind of guy who could fall into a mud puddle and still come up glistening.

The conveyor belt moves us forward and a speaker barks our numbers. We walk through the doors together. Cool nurse hands slide my sweater, my sheepskin boots, my denim knees to the floor. The same hands ebb me into the same as body temperature water. I feel a sleep coming on. My nose is nearly underwater. Bleary eyed, I look over because I want to see him.

He's in the next vat over. Crying. Snotty-faced. There is grayness to his skin, a sort of deadly whitish-bluish pallor. He's being sucked down the drain... Or is he? What is he? Oh, he's lying on something, kind of arched over on his back. The color seems to come back. His cheeks turn pink. His veins pulse.

He stands, dripping and naked. He cries out, "Mother!" She lies there—a husk floating on the water. He tries to hold—to hold—to hold, but she floats tissue-thin on the soap bubbles. He folds her up and rolls her parts as if they are ancient scrolls. When it's all said and done, she's a neat envelope, which he slides into his softer-than-ever briefcase.

Impeccable again, he looks up at the rubber-apron cashier. "How much do I owe you?"

$58.98. The son writes a check. He folds and turns and folds and she becomes a swan. A something that can be held, pirouetted, and viewed. She will be his conversation piece. The cashier bags up a pink tinted bottle. The son uncorks the fat mouth and floats the papyrus bird down. Shakes the bottle sideways until it mimics a ship-in-bottle souvenir. A desk ornament. Message in a bottle.

The water is boiling. I see that now.

I look up. A blue bottle glistens on the floor.

I wake up. I am awake and sweating and Eekin is there.

"You're screaming."

I fling off the covers and grab her hand. I describe the dream—slightly sobbing—slightly laughing.

"What's that supposed to mean?"

I see. She is just my child and it's midnight. As usual, I'm at my wit's end, so I say nothing. I flip on the TV. Flip it back off.

Eekin sits in her crumpled night T-shirt. Three days wrinkled. She looks of hunger. She doesn't ask for food or drink as she starts to shift through architect plans for the add-on couch and the koi pond. She sits cross-legged on the cashmere throw and looks.

Should say something or tell her a story.

I've been waiting days for her to wake and now all I can think of is sleep. Of curling in my wedding quilt. I feel a petulant supermarket tantrum.

TAPE 29
SIDE B

*White House press secretary Tony Snow said Bush hoped to be able
to announce his decisions by Christmas but that the timing could slip.
"It's something that we would like to see, but I'm not going to promise it," Snow said.*
—from "Bush seeks advice on new course in Iraq"
by Ben Fuller, Associated Press

"Who is this woman, here in this picture?" She
waves my birthday picture in the air like a
banner.

"My Memmie," I say.

"And?"

And she had a huge pond in the dip of the pasture at the
bottom of the farm. It was scooped low so she could see it
from the window wall. She had this entire side of the house
glassed and she'd sit there in her leather recliner watching
blue jays and snapping turtles.

Originally, the yard was a slope of crab grass fed by an
underground spring. But things turned desert when her
knees froze into clumsy stone joints and her wrists grew like
pumpkins.

Pap would look up the hill from sawing wood to see her
trapped there in the kitchen, swollen and stranded. She was
marooned in the green felt wallpaper.

Just when she thought it was time to fly off to the ocean,
she froze.

After everything and all that couldn't be helped, there
she was. Twelve kids, miles and miles of weeding, shifting,
raking, and hoeing.

Growing things.

Feeding things.

Selling her fruits to Doctor Baker's first, second, and
third wives at the farmers' market. Every Tuesday for thirty-

five years, she'd tramp her stall with a tub of roasting chickens and lemon grass. She used the money for shoes. So many, many shoes.

She'd wrap her wiry spirals of hair in a red bandanna with a center knot. She told me she couldn't let her mess loose or wives would think she didn't own a brush. The truth is that her hair was wildly impossible to tie down. Waves corkscrewed into tangles up and out from a gray streaked widow's peak. When the wind caught her hair at the nape, it would stand out at right angles every which way. Straight up in swirling static curls.

I don't think it's true what they say. Her hair was alive.

The women in town preferred ironed things, so she'd braid and knot herself for Mary Janes and work boots. She hated the way her corseted hair made her temples ache. She hated the way they called her over to prod the chicken skin or wrap lavender so their gloves would stay white. Mostly she hated the way everything had to be packaged for refrigerator shelves or pantry bins.

She said *the wives* didn't know a thing about freedom. They'd take a perfectly air-dried handkerchief or a pair of starch sprinkled socks and then squash them down into squares. They'd take their long hair and snip it into a straight line. Everything in its place and every place with its thing. *Cleanliness next to godliness.*

They grocery shopped Mondays, laundered linens on Tuesdays.

Ironed on Wednesdays, baked Bundt on Thursdays, Maxine's Beauty Parlor on Fridays, Cary Grant movies on Saturdays, St. Christopher's, First Lutheran, or Brethren's on Sundays.

She was revolutionary. *That woman* didn't fit the unitary order or the hushed swelter. I wouldn't say she was an anarchist, because that is a practice. She was expansive and green. Muddy. Clear. Simple.

She didn't get the constant crimping, curling, folding, dusting.

Who are *they*? What do *they* say?

They were the generation of containers, mothballs, and mapping. They sent their sons to invent Tupperware. Lids that burp. Fake breast milk.

One hundred and one different laundry detergents to dissolve blood and grass stains.

They were sold.

She was ignorant because she couldn't discuss pin curls or girdles. They probably wouldn't have flocked to her but they knew that her chickens were succulent and her herbal tinctures of black cohosh, red clover, wild yam and sarsaparilla could take away the most headaches and cramps.

And she had that pennyroyal tea.

They said it was the roses and dried lavender, but really, it was the fetus tea.

She waited and sold and kept her silence. She tamped wads of money into the little brown basement safe. Planted leafy things between the pear trees. August nights, she slept in the summerhouse with Pap. It was white with open windows, airy and cool, a place where women could cook and not die.

Days he couldn't find her, she was burrowed in the root cellar with the potatoes and Granny Smith apples, sorted into bins according to color and size and perfect roundness. (Civilized ladies want their potatoes medium with few eyes—apples large with curved stems—yams oblong and fat.)

Anything misshapen, crooked, or funky, she caressed and saved for her family. Sometime between December and January, she'd make spectacular apple pies—somehow sweet and sour all in one bite. Her seven boys and five girls refused store pies and kids from town began to show up at the farm on weekends for ice skating and sledding and mostly for her apple pie. It had a wild taste, a sort of zing that made you wish to fly from a cliff or ski off the side of a mountain.

The cinched mothers began to request the recipe, but it could not be duplicated. Pinches and fistfuls of flour were measured by the curves of her knuckles. Brown sugar tossed in like a baseball. Fingery sprinkles of salt. Flour and lard mashed and carved and baked into a crust that reminded of breast milk with its sweet spun tang. Appetites raged. The boys fell in love with their mother, as all boys must surely do.

The daughters fell, too. Into the filigree bite they dove, coming up with an urge to roam off on motorcycles. All five had offers of engagement with rings to match, but it was a long baking winter. Pumpkin pie, cherry, sweet potato, lemon meringue, mincemeat, shoofly, and custard. They were snowed in for days with nothing to do but eat and dream.

She helped them pack suitcases.

Go to the ocean, she whispered into buttermilk bread.

One winter, the children were gone. She moved her woodstove to the attic so she could hear the howling of India winds and the wisp of rain from Vietnam. She stayed there until boys numbered 1, 2, and 3 came home. One without legs, one went crazy, and Johnny was dead. They put their names on a plaque in town.

She switched the pennyroyal out for black tea. Four bastards were born that year to the women of Mayor Bob Henry, Doc Smith, City Councilman Tom Jones, and Postmaster Ed Johnson.

The daughters wrote her from distant lands—Africa, England, and Australia. She couldn't think of what to say back.

The surviving veterans married and brought offerings of new babies, which she'd hold then quickly pass back so she could wander outside for day-long walks—sometimes weeks in the woods.

One day, the crazy one brought her a child with corkscrew black hair.

"She won't stop cryin', Mama."

One month old and wouldn't stop screaming during her dedication at Valley View Bible Church. The pastor said that surely it was some kind of sign. A not necessarily good sign. The boy's new wife was sixteen and rebelling against all things white trash, so she held a black bible as if to wage war. And the revelation began. And she hated this one child because he loved it.

The crazy one told this to Memmie as she looked in my eyes. "Maybe I'd better keep this one for a while."

And the new wife of the crazy one was exhausted from poverty and religion, so she agreed. And the boy said he'd trade the baby for two apple pies. So she baked in July and his eyes got less weird and she strapped the baby on her back with an old cotton bed sheet. Baby me and she walked for days.

Years later, when it was time for school, she sent me back home to a place I'd never known or fit. But they said I should be with my parents. She dropped me off on Sunday nights, picked me up on Fridays.

She was my god. My salvation. My Queen James Version.

When I was six, I saw her hurtle down the side of a snow pile. She was coatless and barefoot and sixty-seven years old as she flung herself backwards and nose-first in an ethereal white glide that ended in a bunch of rolls at the bottom. She had been trapped in the house by a blizzard. Two days of nothing but the Sunday funnies and Parcheesi. Pap had the flu and came downstairs only for coffee. She was restless and would have been long gone if not for me.

The kitchen had a fuzzed sort of stuffed cotton silence. It was as if we were inside a waterless snow globe with the shaking up going on outside. I felt cozy. Mem was cagey, but she knew better than to sneak into the storm because the previous July I'd followed her into the path of a tornado. She said she wasn't scared but she'd hate to see me get swept off too soon.

I was red; she was green. She rolled the dice twice and then said, "Baby, I can't sit here counting squares. Look at these squares and these pegged pieces. They remind me of the plastic market ladies." She told me to stick the game in the burn barrel and grab some newspaper to help her make some kites for spring. We pushed all of the kitchen stuff to the edges of the room so there was this empty open space for creation. She carved the bark off of skinny sticks, which we used to form the ribs of the kites. I measured, cut, and pasted. After that, we tied balls of string to our assortment of fliers and added long leopard tails. She had a pail of barn-red paint. The stuff they painted with during the depression. The red. We also found a bit of yellow, which we dotted over the base coat. By the end of the day, we had seventeen kites of various sizes, which we hung over the kitchen walls—where the pots and pans used to be. The kites hung in a haphazard dance across the room. After every kite was crooked into a jig, she took my hands and spun me round and round until I got the spins. I was so dizzy that I had to lie down to slow the jouncing kites and my eyeballs but not her. She stood, hands on hips, shaking out her head. Jouncing the curls upward. Her fingers seemed to trace waterfalls in the shadows. Tropical corners. Twirling into the shape of wall. Outside.

Sometime while I slept, the storm stopped screaming. It was 2 a.m. So late for a little girl, so early for the queen of dance. I heard her push open the window, where she breathed and breathed in rasping gulps. Then the sound of Pap's voice humming smooth, calming her into the bed. Later, after she died, I asked him about that night, about the deathly silence. He said she had had an urge. The will to run and stay at once. The impossibility of it.

Anyway, as soon as we woke the following morning, she ran outside—well, bolted is more like it. Dashed out in the pink quilted housecoat, flapping like a flamingo walking on water. Scooping up whiteness as she ran. Throwing balls against the Massey Ferguson tractor. I ran back inside to pull on my yellow rubber boots. To catch her. She was gone when I came out, but I could hear her singing in that tone-deaf voice. She only sang outside. AaaaaahAAAAHMAAAa-hizing GraaAAAce OwohOWOH how sweet theahea sound. Sang like a banshee. Came back five days later. Took me to her boy. Went hiking for a year.

This was my life.

Then one day her legs stopped moving. We had to do something, but what? What to do? Looking back now, I don't quite remember how or when she became immobile. One day I was young and she was immortal. We knelt together in the mint and basil. She ebbed and throbbed with our lives in her hand. We suckled. Graded dirt. Plucked earthworms. Beautiful grandearthmother goddess woman. She was someone you'd imagine walking up from the center of the earth. A golden eagle swooping home with silvery fish between her teeth, breathing life into chicks and peas. Other times, spiriting away without a sound.

She spent days speaking without words. Her eyes drifted between cupboards and the wooden garden swing. Up and back. Searching to teach me this bodyspeak language.

Laughing with the dead boy. Planting useless things like daisies and dandelions. Plaiting onion tails and radishes. Eating earth with a spoon to satiate the need to crunch to make a sound. To be definite.

I remember seeing her there inside the six-paned room on the eastern side of the house. She was hobbled by crippling arthritis. Hanging by a thread. Lying against the window. Sort of standing, sort of falling. Sort of dying into the spring. Not breathing. Crying. I thought she saw me coming from the bus. She was waving, but not to me. Her hands were against the glass, swirling towards the oak and cherry trees. They would not blossom that spring. Wretched and pink. Scraggly.

I ran in then. Afraid to speak. I stood at the window and saw the hateful wheelchair up to its spokes in mud. I lined a wheelbarrow with sheepskin and wheeled her to the garden, where I tipped her gently into the hillside. Her hair had lost its verve. Scraped back from the shrill widow's peak, flat against her head. Her eyes roved like the crazy son. Screaming. Screaming *no*, I loosened the knot at the nape of her neck. I fluffed her hair into the breeze and out. Then I went to the metal chair and buried it under a mound of dirt. A tawny hill planted with forsythia seedlings and a hellchair.

I brought her offerings of garter snakes and baby rabbits in shoebox houses. We grew tomato and bean sprouts on the window ledge. She began to crave crippled things. Crows with broken wings. Cracked robin eggs. A baby calf that'd broken its leg.

Herbs and casts.

Bone mending.

Every day, she'd ask for a new window. A place that had to be cut from the wall to reveal a thing she couldn't see. I became adept at sawing. Many of the windows were oddly shaped.

Circles.

Triangles.

Hexagons.

Every window had to be opened during rainstorms.

She stopped sleeping, as if to dare her heart to wear out. Keep up, you beating bastard. Keep up.

The pain moved to her hips and fingers.

I built a wagon waist-high with fat tractor wheels so we could navigate her gardens.

Take me to the woods.

I'd cover her in flowers and leaves and she'd lie there as I planted, weeded and watered. I gave her pots of earth. She sunk her fingers in and swirled. I sprinkled her sweat on lettuce heads. Her touch was a potion.

I read her books about buffaloes and six-shooters. Mostly Louis L'Amour. Once I tried to read Bronte, but she didn't get it. She wanted then. The way we want things when time has gone and the want becomes a rust in the joints. It wants a self to inhabit. To fuck wide open on the range. She wanted cowboy stories. Horses and leather. Wild men. Breasty women.

We hid the books under her blanket when Pap came home from work.

He wasn't much on fiction. Thought it was a waste of time. I guess you could say he wasn't much of a valentine man—more like a cracked leather boot. Fitted and soft on the inside.

Every night, I made him dinner like she told me. Some kind of meat with some kind of potatoes, maybe corn, always two slices of buttered bread with grape jelly. He had a way of eating that made you want to cook more. Head down. Intent upon the spoon. Spearing things with forks. He never talked until the food was gone, and then it was mostly about the office boys. He always called them boys, even if they were older than he was. Those college boys with flabby rear ends and sparkling fingernails. Make you feel dumber than dumb. The ones who get hour-long lunches to rest from the effort of sitting down. Well, he thought that was the grand hoax of all time. Getting paid to sit at a clean pressed desk. He had a sort of disdainful envy towards the boys. A wishful wanting to sparkle.

I told him I thought bulldozing things up and down was much better. After all, who wants to add numbers and write names on lines? Boring. He'd look at the axle grease under his blunt fingernails and then sort of jam them into his pockets or underneath the tablecloth. "They never really come clean, you know." I'd nod and wouldn't know what to say to that one, so I'd stare at him through the bottom of my water glass. His eyes slanted down to me, his mouth magnified, as if swollen from so much chow. He smelled of leaves and rubber. Outdoor working things.

Those damn fingernails. That was the big deal because one time he went to deposit his check at the one bank in town. There was this scrawny teller man with the name Frank tagged to his chest. He wore a pressed cotton shirt and a skinny green tie. He took Pap's check and gave a tepid sniff, which Pap assumed to be a token of disgust over his hands. All the way home, he bitched. "My pay's six times that little fella's... Probably can't even change a tire... Funny little man..." He was humiliated. Every payday after that, he made me take the check inside the bank in a crinkled envelope.

He wasn't fancy or much of a dancer. But he wanted to be. One of them.

Astaire, Grant, or Stewart. Tipping over ladder-back chairs. Floating in tailcoats. High haberdashery in top hats and snowy white shirttails.

A sculptor. He was familiar with mud and straw. An expert digger of holes and caverns. An above-the-ground tunnel rat. Grooving in the trenches. Talking to himself about mouths to feed. Shoes to buy. Holes and mounds became velvet-roped hotels and ponderous banks. Digging was all he knew.

So that's what he did for Memmie when the time came— when she couldn't get out. She who loved growing things in soil. She who saw poetry in his eyes and cowboy on his lips.

Every day, he'd remember when they met. In the dirt by the side of the new railroad restaurant that was going up beside the Susquehanna. He was shirtless, covered in dust.

She was 19 to his 17. Neither one was looking for anything. She dreamed of gritty solitude somewhere by the water. He dreamed of hot baths. She had Granny Smith apples in a basket. He was scrawling words into the limestone rock. Her hair was crawling out of its stoic braid and creeping upward like a helium octopus. His eyes were amber and full of chaps. Her skin was silk leather. His hands were good at filling things.

He stopped writing. She came inside.

Now forty years later and what did he know?

1. Baseball means something.
2. You can work yourself to death.
3. Twelve kids are too many.
4. There will be no life after this.

He got desperate.

So when her hips locked into rusted sockets, he tried church. Went to where the crazy boy spent Sundays and Wednesdays. Crept into the back row in a suit that bagged around the ass. Listened to the organ wailing a hymn from page 452 and then a sermon about St. John. Shook hands with the collared man and begged for a miracle. The man was Pastor Randolph. He explained that membership was equal to the cost of a pew. Tax deductible. Pap kicked a dust ball and rolled a cigarette.

Back home, he sat on the edge of his yellow bulldozer and smoked an entire pouch of Red Man tobacco. He imagined his mangled words flowing up somehow, inside the cherry mist of the leaves. He thought about her hair smoking up, just like in 1932. He thought about knowing and the idea of gods and salvation and the price of things. He thought about doctors and how she hated the cold. He thought about the way he smoothed sonnets on her neck and how she put flowers on his rollaway desk—the one he was too exhausted to use.

Helpless.

Then he thought about craters and dynamite and the first day she saw him, as if he were a sculpture of some Greek god. That's what she said. Lying there. Tracing his biceps and the skin at the backs of his knees.

She never saw the ocean!

He started to dig.

By the end of the day, he had carved the north pasture into an oblong thigh of water. I sat there and watched the Caterpillar claw and dump tangles of dandelion roots and crabgrass into hairy mounds.

She watched this last poem from her window. Pinioned to her chair at the hips. Joints burning and bumming. Oh. Not so much was the pain, for that could be ignored. No, this was a shutdown. A lack of movement. The smearing of a lightning bug. Things were melting. Fusing together near the backbone. Movement became rigid and lumpy. She said she felt corseted like the wives.

I went down to help with the digging. Together, we screamed into the maw of earth.

Blisters grew on top of blisters.

The pond took a few weeks to fill with water. Fresh water burbled into the hole from an underground spring in measures of teaspoons and cups, but by mid-July, it was filling enough to be measured. Pap tied an arrowhead at the end of the string. This he dropped and then held straight to find depth. After he was done, I would ball up the string and stick it into the heart of my favorite willow tree.

I loved that tree. It was like one of those bubble umbrellas that come down over your head and shoulders. The only thing getting wet in those things was the feet. I guess they don't make them anymore. Too many people tripped and sued.

Finally, on August 29th it was deep enough to float things, so he went to the Gratz auction and bought a bunch of white ducks and freshwater bass stock. He folded the animals into the water like walnuts into a batter, then he lay on the handmade dock and stirred them in with an oar. I brought a box of lily pads from a small pond in the back woods. We laid the binoculars beside Memmie so she could look for snakes and muskrats.

Trapped as she was, we resorted to chemicals. Darkrooms and photo trays. Tripods to sit just inside here to capture outside there. Clotheslines hung in the papered room. Pictures of grass hanging limply. Nothing but fields and fields of grass. Squares pinned side by side as if they were sod.

They waved and rolled.

She called them her wheat poems. Hours and hours spent watching the tallest strand stretching up—lifting the brownish beetle into the blue. Daddy long-leggers became fascinating. "Things with roots can't fly," she said. It was a Thursday night about seven. I had wheeled her out beside the greenhouse into a corner facing the water. The crabgrass itched and squirmed beneath me, but I tried to be silent as she reminded me of childish things.

She rolled a punk between her teeth. "When I was six years old, I had this doll named Sally. She was golden with blue glass eyes. Daddy brought her back from Atlantic City. He worked there one summer. Every fourth weekend, he'd come home on the train to tell us about the candy booths and dancing ocean elephants. In New Jersey? We couldn't believe it! Daddy said there were weird things. Fascinating. He didn't own a suit, so he'd float after dark in his underclothes. He said the waves could rock you like a big momma. He wasn't great at describing things, but I could see his eyes daze off like liquid, which made me know that I had to get there. But then I had all those babies and now it's 1972 and the people on the TV just stand there in the ocean in bras and panties or get eaten by sharks. I couldn't do that."

I felt like crying then because she wanted to be six again with her salty daddy. She kept Sally wrapped in a suitcase with a homemade swimsuit, a silver harmonica, and a brass clasped purse. These are the things she'd packed for the ocean on that day when she met him.

She never told Pap, but the day they met, she'd been headed to Jersey, where she planned to work and buy a cottage. She never dreamed of marriage.

So there she was, walking along and into him, all muddied and full of poetry. And so the 1:50 train to Philly steamed off without her.

TAPE 30
SIDE A

Terrorolympics—Bullet Proof Punk. Osama catches bullets with his teeth.

—a game posted on AddictingGames.com

Eekin is gone. I looked up just now, and she's gone. My Grandma stories are too long.

By the way, Dr. Jones, I haven't received my January billing. You can email me, if you like.

I wish she'd said goodbye. Maybe she did. I'm not a great listener. I don't know... I sort of thought the story would help. It's something I think of constantly.

That love is a retelling—a something in the back of my head. A something I keep or kept or try to get to. Get back to as if I had it but never did, which is what confuses me. It's a wish to be poetry. Some kind of sonnet striation through the being of a thing. It's that one piece of work you read over and over and crease into the pocket of your favorite jeans until the parchment merges with your skin to become a pulse. It's a wanting to be part of something larger. Something communal. A nesting beneath the skin of another. A burial.

That's how it should be or was in her story. But isn't. Rarely is anything in mine.

Little things.

Shot glasses.

Most times, the story is like a New Orleans strip bar. You know, the little ones nestled in the bottoms of white-washed brick-stone buildings built in the 1800s. They promise fresh pussy with a bottle of whiskey, but then you get past the door and it's all reeky bodies and sticky tables. So old and so anciently sickening and full of piss. You want to die for the sad ageless women spinning there in their caked-on makeup. Their eyes look and look beyond and up just past the last row of lolling bodies and they see nothing more than more and more and more legs and arms all scratching-stretching for a better crotch shot.

I've been drawn into those stony places like a calling to church. To minister. All that promise and hope at the shiny front door, which you can rarely see beyond. So you give your money for a front row pew to hear about sinners.

Crosses and poles.

Bourbon Street with its outside competition. Stupid little college girls flashing their titties for plastic beads. Drunk and seamless. Everything so shiny and ooohLAla.

Middle-aged couples in khaki pressed pants and brown lettered bags. *L* and *V*, as if to mean something. Days worked? You're Republican? What? Cocked there at odd angles, trying not to be interested but oh so wet. Oh, the grinding asses and carpets and bones on dollar bills. Clit, oh show me some clitoris. Illegal, yes. But OH. Do show. Pull aside your panties so I can dream of licking you raw in the raw. I'll take my wife home. My husband home. Fuck 'em like it's you. Cook me some bacon and eggs. Fold some turkey and Swiss onto my collarbone.

The children are hungry. Must pack lunches.

She knows. She, the woman without the lettered bag. The one who carries canvas and smokes unlabeled cigarettes. In stilts and pasties, she wiggles. She's the one you think you want. Vodka smooth and clear. Everything is OK.

It is, isn't it?

The bills are paid on time, aren't they?

She.

She.

Girl one snorts coke to forget the dry heaves.

Girl two swallows Prozac with her Starbucks.

Girl one squeezes oranges for him in the big bay house with the leather divan.

Girl two squeezes baby oil between her legs to pay the electric and water.

Girl one makes no money of her own.

Girl two brings in four or five hundred a night.

Girl one is living on borrowed time. Wrinkles come due in balloon payments when you've got nothing left but senseless jewelry.

Girl two will probably be dead or crazy by the time her ass starts sagging.

Girl one will buy Botox. She'll pray it does the trick.

Girl two will get the boot. She'll wait tables at truck stops.

Booty call one.

Booty call two.

Eyes jawing out from the sockets. Rip her out, tear her out, away out!

Each clawing the other, sister to sister to mother to daughter and bawling and boning.

He pays for girl one's drinks.

He tips girl two.

He walks out with one.

He looks back at two.

Girl one gets to carry the platinum AmEx.

Girl two gets a hundred-dollar tip.

At home, she rubs herself and spreads in search of heat.

The batteries are dead.

TAPE 30
SIDE B

Journalism is all about conveying to the masses any significant development in politics, finance, defense or the society as a whole. Journalism is an ethic-driven career; therefore it demands a high level of personal discipline and a burning desire to communicate with the masses and go against all odds to present the people with news as it is.
  —as defined at www.unixl.com/dir/humanities/journalism/

I love New Orleans cross dressers, whores, and soccer moms. I love the homeless guy who plays trombone for paper bag forties. I love the polyester lady in the catfish place and the way she scratches her titties before writing 2 small Pepsi and a fries. I love the church that smells like ass.

I love the way we drank so much tequila that Bob Dylan's cowboy hat looked like a loaf of bread. But he sang and I got those goosebumps on my arms and belly. And you said throw it up there. And I said what, you want me to throw up? And you said no the bra. Throw the bra at his bread and we'll take pictures and eat rum pudding. So I did and he didn't miss a beat; crooked his bendy voice and hanked a wail of words hard and sweet. And no one could move after that. And even nonsmokers sucked one. And for a very long time, we felt what needed to be said. There it was quivering in the air, lifting up on the voice of the kind of man it takes to say a thing like that.

The sky is full of haiku and rambles. That's what he said. That's what did it. The beauty we'd missed by working out the balance at the bottom of the sheets.

And then I didn't know where to buy a bra at the jazz fest. So I bobbled like all the others. Beaded. Strung. Smoked. Changed.

I need to fix that. Be one or the other. Not these halves. There is too much to think, to do, to throw. This business.

Those babies. Eekin. The perfume. The cancer. Thanksgiving. Easter.

The fact that batteries are not included with this purchase.